Girls' Weekend Survival

Cynthia Hickey

The Sheriff of Misty Hollow, Book 1

ISBN-13: 978-1-965352-23-6

To my friends, Ramona, Frankina, Patricia, Amanda, and to our girls' weekends that, thankfully, do not turn out like this one. Love you, girls.

Contents

Chapter One

Shea Callahan tossed a battered duffel bag and backpack into the back of the rental van her soccer mom friend Becky had rented and winced. A girl's weekend in the mountains should be a welcome retreat, but her mind wouldn't stop straying to how the folks of Misty Hollow would react to their new sheriff being a woman. She unzipped the bag, checked her handgun, then zipped the bag back up and closed the back of the van. Would the residents of Misty Hollow think she could handle the rash of crime that had plagued the town the last few years?

The weight of the badge in her jacket pocket felt heavier than it should. She'd spent the last three years as a deputy in a county where the good ole boys made it clear that women belonged at home, not wearing a uniform. Then a detective before that. The snide comments, the deliberate exclusion from important cases, the way they'd talk over her during briefings—all of it had worn her down. Misty Hollow represented a fresh start, a chance to prove herself without the baggage of preconceived notions.

"That's the last of it." Becky grinned and opened the driver's side door. "You sure you don't want to drive?"

"I'll take the next shift." She glanced at the mound of luggage. Way too much for a simple weekend away. Emma alone had brought three suitcases, claiming she needed options for every possible weather scenario and social situation they might encounter.

"Got your inhaler?"

Shea frowned. "Yes, Mom." The asthma had been a constant companion since childhood, triggered by stress and high altitudes. Not exactly ideal traits for someone about to become sheriff of a mountain town. She'd learned to manage it, always keeping her rescue inhaler close and her maintenance medication routine strict.

"Sorry. It's a habit." Becky grinned. "I can't help myself. I've been mothering you all since we were eighteen."

"I'm so glad we managed to do this." Emma, the cheerleader of the group, slid into the backseat. "The ten of us have talked about this since college. It's about time, don't you think?" Her perfectly styled blonde hair bounced as she settled in, already pulling out her phone to document the beginning of their adventure.

Tessa, expensive braids swinging, climbed in next.

"I have to admit to being a bit nervous to stay on Misty Mountain. Too many things have happened up there." She glanced back at Shea. "You sure you want to work in that town?" Her voice carried the concern of someone who'd grown up hearing stories about the strange happenings in small mountain communities.

"I'm sure." After the way good ole Southern boys treated a woman deputy, a small, secluded town sounded perfect. Hopefully, she could prove her worth without prejudice. She tied her long, dark hair into a messy bun, then climbed into the front passenger seat since she never failed to get car sick in the back. She felt her pocket to make sure she hadn't forgotten her inhaler, then clicked her seatbelt into place.

The familiar ritual of checking for her medication had become second nature over the years. Her father, a retired cop himself, had always told her that preparation was the key to survival in law enforcement. "Know your weaknesses," he'd said, "and make sure they never become liabilities." The asthma was manageable as long as she stayed vigilant.

"Yay!" Becky started the engine. "This weekend is going to be great."

Despite wishing she could spend the next few days preparing for her new job, Shea smiled. She loved these women and would do her best to focus on having a good time with them. They'd been her anchor through college, the sisters she'd never had growing up as an only child in a military household that moved every few years.

"Shea, Tessa, Becky, Lauren, Melanie, Annie, Deborah, Kara, Rachel, and me," Emma counted. "The terrific ten set loose upon the world."

"I think that happened at graduation." Deborah, the serious one, stared at her phone. "Will we have service on that mountain?" As a financial advisor, she couldn't afford to be completely disconnected from her clients, even for a weekend.

Shea doubted it. "No idea. All I know is that we've rented a large cabin overlooking the valley." The place had looked gorgeous online. Five bedrooms, three bathrooms, a full kitchen, and a hot tub on the deck. The price had seemed too good to be true, which should have been her first red flag.

"I think it's going to storm most of the time." Rachel tended to look on the dark side of things. She'd been the same way in college, always expecting the worst possible outcome in every situation. Somehow, her pessimism had served her well as a risk assessment specialist for an insurance company.

"No, it won't." Emma shook her head. "I won't allow it to. This weekend is going to be perfect." She'd already planned activities for every possible scenario—hiking if it was sunny, board games if it rained, and group meditation sessions regardless of weather.

If the growing excitement in the van as they neared Misty Hollow was any indication, the weekend would be just as they all hoped. A time to reminisce, reconnect, and maybe relive a little of their college days when the ten of them had been inseparable. Since graduation, most of their contact took place online. Text messages, social media likes, and the occasional video call had replaced the daily interactions they'd once shared.

Shea leaned her head back and closed her eyes, content to listen as the others chattered about marriage and babies. Neither of which she had anything to add. While her friends had settled into domestic life, she'd thrown herself into her career, determined to break through the barriers that kept women from advancing in law enforcement.

The conversation drifted to memories of their college days—late-night study sessions, spring break adventures, and the drama that had seemed so important at the time. Lauren reminisced about her disastrous relationship with a philosophy major who'd convinced her to dye her hair purple. Melanie laughed about the time they'd all gotten food poisoning from a sketchy taco truck but had still insisted on going to the homecoming dance.

Misty Hollow's former sheriff, a man named Westbrook, had congratulated Shea on the fact no one ran against her. Why was that? No one knew her there from Adam. She'd contacted Westbrook upon hearing of his retirement, sent in some letters of recommendation, gave a speech, and the next thing she knew, she wore a star on her chest.

The whole process had been surprisingly smooth, almost suspiciously so. In her experience, sheriff positions were highly competitive, especially in small towns where everyone knew everyone else's business. The fact that she'd essentially waltzed into the job with minimal opposition made her wonder what she was walking into.

If she were honest with herself, the whole situation left her apprehensive. Plus, a couple of the deputies had left when Westbrook retired which meant Shea also had to find replacements. One more reason she needed to be at work and not on the top of a mountain. The department would be severely understaffed when she started, and she'd be working with people who might resent having an outsider—and a woman—as their new boss.

"I can hear your brain from here," Becky said. "You aren't supposed to report to the office until Monday. Enjoy the next three days, okay?"

She cracked one eye open. "I'm trying." The truth was, she'd never been good at turning off her analytical mind. Even in college, she'd been the one who studied while her friends partied, who worried about finals while others assumed everything would work out.

"You always were the serious one." Becky patted Shea's leg. "You really need to learn to relax."

"I was relaxing until you started talking." Shea grinned to take the sting out of her words. The banter felt good, familiar. These women knew her better than anyone, had seen her at her worst and still loved her anyway.

Her friend giggled. "Maybe you'll find a man in Misty Hollow. One that can handle your moodiness."

"Ha, ha." Shea didn't have time for romance. Her career took up too much of her time and that's the way she preferred her life to be. Men only complicated things. She'd learned that lesson the hard way with her last relationship, when her ex-boyfriend had made it clear that he expected her to choose between him and her job. The choice had been easy, but it had still hurt.

The van wound through increasingly narrow mountain roads, the scenery growing more dramatic with each mile. Pine trees stretched toward the sky, their branches creating a canopy that filtered the afternoon sunlight into dancing patterns on the asphalt. The air grew thinner, and Shea felt the familiar tightness in her chest that meant her body was adjusting to the altitude.

"I'm going to stop here to get gas." Becky turned in front of a small, one pump gas station. "We're headed up the mountain from here."

The station looked like something from a bygone era—weathered wood siding, a hand-painted sign, and a single ancient pump that probably hadn't been updated since the 1980s. A few pickup trucks were parked off to the side, their occupants nowhere to be seen.

"I didn't see the town." Annie peered out the window, her voice tinged with disappointment. She'd been hoping to do some antiquing, convinced that small mountain towns were treasure troves of vintage finds.

"We're on the opposite side of Misty Mountain," Shea explained. "Going through the town would've added time to our drive." She shoved her door open. "I'll take care of the gas since you've driven the whole way."

"You don't have to do that, but thanks." Becky smiled, already stretching her arms above her head to work out the kinks from the long drive.

Shea exited the van and filled the tank, her law enforcement training automatically cataloging details about their surroundings. The isolation of the location, the lack of visible security cameras, the fact that they hadn't seen another vehicle for the last twenty minutes. Old habits died hard, and she'd learned to trust her instincts about potentially dangerous situations.

She started to pay with her card and noticed the sign that said to pay inside. Great. She'd get caught up into a conversation with a most likely bored employee who'd want to know their entire life story.

The aroma of fried chicken and hot pizza greeted her as she pushed open the door. The interior was dimly lit, with narrow aisles crammed full of snacks, drinks, and basic supplies. A small deli counter occupied one corner, where the promised fried chicken sat under heat lamps. She pasted on a smile and approached the counter. "I'm here to pay for the gas."

The middle-aged man in denim overalls peered

around her, his eyes scanning the van and its occupants with obvious curiosity. "Where y'all headed?" His accent was thick, the words drawled out in the way of people who'd never lived anywhere but these mountains.

Shea slapped forty dollars on the counter. "We've rented a cabin on Eagle's Bluff." She kept her voice neutral, professional. Something about the man's intense scrutiny made her uncomfortable, though she couldn't put her finger on exactly why.

His eyebrows rose, and for a moment, something that looked like concern flickered across his weathered features. "Folks don't go up that way much. Haven't in a long time."

"Why not? The photos looked gorgeous." The rental listing had been full of pristine images— sweeping valley views, pristine forest surroundings, and a deck that seemed to float above the treetops.

"Oh, it's pretty enough." He rang up the gas and handed her change, his movements deliberate and slow. "Real pretty. That's not the problem."

Shea waited for him to say more. For several seconds, they stood and stared at each other, the silence stretching uncomfortably between them. The only sounds were the hum of the refrigerated cases and the distant murmur of voices from somewhere in the back of the store.

"You gals be careful up there," he finally said, his voice carrying a weight that seemed disproportionate to the simple words.

"Wild animals?" Shea asked, though she suspected that wasn't what he was worried about.

"Something like that." His gaze bore into hers, and she got the distinct impression he was trying to communicate something without saying it outright.

Again, she expected him to say more. She almost identified herself as the new sheriff but decided against it. This weekend she was only Shea Callahan, not Sheriff Callahan. She needed these few days to be just a woman enjoying time with her friends, not a law enforcement officer constantly on duty.

"You gals come try out our pizza if you don't want to cook. You won't be sorry." The sudden shift to a more cheerful tone felt forced, as if he'd remembered he was supposed to be welcoming to potential customers.

"Thanks." Shea flashed a smile and left the store. The back of her neck prickled, and she glanced back to see the man staring after her through the window. She shuddered, remembering stories about the strangeness of mountain folk. Her father had always said that isolation did things to people, made them suspicious of outsiders and protective of secrets that might be better shared.

The man turned away first and said something to someone she couldn't see. Another voice responded, too low for her to make out the words, but the tone seemed urgent. Her law enforcement instinct left her feeling uneasy, that familiar tingle that told her something wasn't quite right about the situation.

She slid back into the van, her mind already cataloging the details she'd observed—the man's nervous energy, the way he'd avoided giving her a straight answer about why people didn't visit Eagle's Bluff, the fact that he'd seemed genuinely concerned for their safety.

"Let's get out of here. Folks are strange." She tried to keep her voice light, not wanting to alarm her friends with her growing unease.

Becky shot her a questioning look. "What is that smell?"

"Fried chicken and pizza." Despite her discomfort with the man's behavior, she had to admit the food had smelled incredible. Her stomach growled, reminding her that they'd been on the road for hours with nothing but gas station snacks.

"Oh, good. We know where to eat tonight. I'm sure no one feels like cooking after the long drive." She pulled from the station and continued up the mountain, the van's engine working harder as the grade increased.

"I don't eat pizza," Emma said from the backseat. "Too many carbs."

"Carbs don't count on girl's weekend," Rachel said from the back. "Everyone knows that."

Laughter erupted as the others agreed, the mood lightening as they left the strange encounter behind. Shea tried to shake off her unease, telling herself she was being paranoid. Just because she was used to looking for trouble didn't mean it existed everywhere she went.

The road grew narrower and more winding as they climbed higher, the drop-offs becoming more dramatic with each turn. Through the trees, she caught glimpses of the valley below, a patchwork of fields and forests that stretched to the horizon. It really was beautiful up here, she had to admit.

They arrived at a large A-frame cabin on the side of a bluff. A back deck hung over where the ground steeply sloped toward the cliff. The structure was impressive, all natural wood and glass, designed to take full advantage of the spectacular views.

"It's beautiful. I have no idea why no one comes here." Shea glanced around the heavily wooded area. A creek babbled not far from the cabin, its sound creating a peaceful backdrop that should have been soothing. Instead, the isolation felt oppressive, the silence between the creek's murmurs too complete.

"What do you mean no one comes here?" Tessa narrowed her eyes. "It's way more secluded than I thought. We haven't passed another house for miles. It's kind of spooky, and we're going to be here for three days."

The realization hit all of them at once—they truly were alone up here. No neighbors to call for help, no cell phone service, no easy way to get assistance if something went wrong. The nearest town was at least an hour's drive down treacherous mountain roads.

Shea shrugged, trying to project more confidence than she felt. "The man at the gas station seemed surprised we were coming here. He said no one comes here anymore." It couldn't be the price, because it had been ridiculously low for such a place. In hindsight, that should have been another warning sign.

She'd thought they were getting a good deal when Becky sent her the link. Now she wasn't so sure. A shadow hovered over the beauty of the place, something intangible but unmistakable. Even her friends had quieted, their earlier excitement dimmed by the realization of just how isolated they were.

Whether from the same feeling that something wasn't quite right, or simply because they were in awe of the scenery, the mood had shifted. The chatter died down as they gathered their luggage, each woman lost in her own thoughts as they prepared to spend the next few days in this beautiful but eerily empty place.

Shea hoped they wouldn't regret their decision to come. Their long weekend could be longer than any of them wanted, and she couldn't shake the feeling that they'd walked into something they didn't understand. As the new sheriff of Misty Hollow, she was supposed to protect people from danger—but what happened when the danger was something she couldn't identify or prepare for?

The mountain seemed to watch them unpack, keeping its secrets close while the wind whispered warnings through the pines.

Chapter Two

They should've picked up pizza when they were at the station. Shea shoved the things from her bag into the top drawer of one of the dressers. They could've warmed it up in the oven. Now, rather than relax with a glass of wine on the deck, she was going to head back with Becky.

She glanced in the corner of the bedroom where a small security camera nestled. Its lack of a glowing light told her that it most likely didn't work without Wi-Fi. So, why install them? Unless the cabin owner planned on having Wi-Fi one day. The more she thought about it, the stranger it seemed. Who put security cameras in a rental cabin that had no internet connection? The device looked expensive, professional-grade, not the kind of cheap deterrent most property owners used.

She examined the camera more closely, noting its positioning gave it a clear view of the entire room. A chill ran down her spine as she realized there were probably cameras in all the bedrooms. She made a mental note to check the other rooms and warn her friends. Privacy was one thing, but this felt invasive, even voyeuristic.

"Here you go." Her friend tossed her a bright pink tee shirt.

Shea caught it in one hand, then held it up to read the writing on the front. A picture of a cabin in the woods and the words Girl's Weekend. "You expect me to wear this?" The shirt was aggressively feminine, with sparkly letters and cartoon images that made her feel like she was dressing up for a sorority mixer.

"You can't always wear black." Becky grinned and left, no doubt to hand out the other shirts. She ducked back into the room. "Wearing it is mandatory. We leave to pick up supper in ten minutes."

"Ugh." Shea changed from her black tee into the pink one. Why were all her friends so girly? Please don't let anyone in the Misty Hollow sheriff's office see her wearing this. They'd never take her seriously. The fabric felt foreign against her skin, too bright, too cheerful for someone who lived in muted colors and practical clothing.

She caught her reflection in the dresser mirror and winced. The pink shirt clashed with her dark hair and serious expression, making her look like she was playing dress-up in someone else's clothes. But Becky had planned this weekend down to the last detail, and wearing matching shirts was apparently part of the experience.

"Why me?" She asked, settling into the van.

"No one else wanted to come. Besides…I haven't talked to you in ages." Becky's voice carried a weight that Shea hadn't noticed before, something beneath the usual cheerful exterior.

"We're both busy, Becky. I'm sorry." The guilt hit her immediately. While she'd been focused on her career, her friends had been living their lives, dealing with problems she hadn't even known about.

"I'm not blaming you." She sighed and backed away from the cabin. "I wanted to speak with you in private. There won't be a lot of privacy this weekend."

Uh-oh. "What's wrong?" Shea braced herself. In her experience, when someone needed privacy to share news, it was rarely good.

"Bill and I have separated." She cleared her throat, eyes blinking rapidly. "He wants more. Says I spend too much time with the boys and not enough time with him. How does he think separating will change that is what I'd like to know. Not living together means less time spent with him, right?"

The words tumbled out in a rush, as if Becky had been holding them back for weeks. Shea could hear the pain beneath her friend's attempt at levity, the confusion of someone trying to make sense of a relationship falling apart.

"I'm sorry." Shea put a hand on her friend's arm. "Anything I can do?" She felt helpless, trained to solve crimes and catch criminals but completely unprepared to offer relationship advice.

"Arrest him for being an idiot?" A chuckle turned into a sob. "I wanted to let you know. I didn't want to ruin everyone else's weekend by breaking down in front of them."

"Forget about him. This weekend is for us girls." The words felt inadequate, but Shea wasn't sure what else to say. She'd never been good at the emotional support thing, preferring action to words.

"Right." She turned toward the gas station. "The pizza should be ready. I called it in ahead of time."

"Organized as always." Shea tried to inject some warmth into her voice. Becky had always been the planner, the one who kept their group connected, who remembered birthdays and organized reunions. It seemed wrong that her marriage was falling apart while she was trying so hard to take care of everyone else.

"With three boys, I have to be." She cut off the engine. "Don't tell the others, okay? They all think I have everything together."

"You do have it all together. This is just a bump in the road." Shea pushed open her door, wishing she could knock some sense into Bill. The man had a wife who would move mountains for the people she loved, and he was too blind to see it.

The same group of men loitered near the door of the gas station. More had joined them since earlier, their voices carrying across the parking lot in rough laughter and crude comments. One, a rough-looking man wearing a trucker hat, dirty jeans, and a stained T-shirt, tipped his hat. "Ladies." His gaze fell to Shea's chest, lingering on the ridiculous pink shirt in a way that made her skin crawl.

She nodded curtly, brushing past him and into the station. The man's look gave her the creeps. She'd dealt with men like this before—the kind who saw women as objects, who mistook politeness for invitation. Her hand instinctively moved toward her hip, where her service weapon usually rested, but found nothing but the soft fabric of her civilian clothes.

"Talk about being undressed by someone's eyes." Becky glared over her shoulder, her voice tight with disgust.

"I don't like the fact we've just advertised to a group of rough looking hillbillies that we're a group of women alone." She glanced at the cash register, remembering her earlier conversation with the attendant. She'd told the man there earlier exactly where they were all staying. The information had seemed harmless at the time, but now it felt like a mistake.

The inside of the station felt different now, more threatening. The narrow aisles that had seemed quaint earlier felt like potential traps, places where someone could corner them. The smell of fried food that had been appetizing before seemed cloying, mixing with the scent of motor oil and cigarette smoke in a way that made her stomach turn.

While Becky picked up the pizza, Shea kept a close watch on the group of men outside. Her law enforcement training kicked in automatically, cataloging details—how many men, their approximate ages and sizes, whether any of them appeared to be armed. Her stomach twisted into knots as the man in the cap met her stare through the window. A slow grin spread under his beard, revealing yellowed teeth. This man was trouble.

"The door." Becky, arms piled with four pizzas headed toward her.

Shea opened the door and let her step out first, positioning herself between her friend and the group of men. The protective instinct was automatic, honed by years of training and experience.

"Nice shirts," ball cap said, his voice carrying easily across the small space. "Gonna be a fun weekend, huh?" His voice was low, mocking, with an undertone that made Shea's skin crawl.

Becky gave a nervous giggle and increased her pace toward the van, practically stumbling in her haste to get away from the men's leering stares. "Shea?"

"Coming." The man was definitely not harmless. More predatory than she'd first thought. The way he looked at them wasn't just rude—it was calculating, as if he was assessing them for some purpose she didn't want to consider.

As she and Becky drove away, she glanced in the sideview mirror. The group of men had stepped onto the road, watching as the van drove away. One of them pulled out a cell phone, and she saw him gesturing toward their retreating vehicle. Yep. She and Becky had attracted the wrong kind of attention.

"Did you see that?" Becky's voice was shaky. "The way they were looking at us?"

"I saw." Shea's jaw tightened. "When we get back to the cabin, we need to talk to the others about staying alert."

"You're scaring me."

"Good. A little healthy fear might keep us all safe." The words came out harsher than she'd intended, but she was running on adrenaline now, her protective instincts in full gear.

Back at the cabin, the mood was lighter. The other women had spent the time unpacking and exploring, claiming bedrooms and admiring the view from the deck. As soon as the pizzas were set on the dining table, wine was poured, and the earlier tension seemed to evaporate.

"To a great weekend away." Emma raised her glass in a toast, her blonde hair catching the light from the chandelier.

The others followed suit, then carried plates with slices of pizza and their glasses to the back deck. A full moon lit up the area, casting everything in silver light that should have been romantic but somehow felt ominous. A soft breeze blew over the valley, carrying with it the scent of pine and something else—something earthy and slightly unpleasant that Shea couldn't identify.

"You really are moving to a beautiful part of the state, Shea," Annie said, settling into one of the deck chairs with her wine. "Even if you'll be down there instead of up here on the mountain."

She agreed. The area was indeed gorgeous, if a bit overgrown. But beauty could hide danger, as she'd learned in her years of law enforcement. Some of the most horrific crimes she'd investigated had taken place in locations that looked like postcards.

A twig snapped below them, and she froze, her entire body going on alert. The sound was distinct, deliberate, not the random noise of wind through branches. She waited, listening intently, relaxing only when no other sound came. The encounter at the gas station had left her on edge, every sense heightened and ready for trouble.

Was that a footstep? The sound had been too heavy, too purposeful for a small animal. She got to her feet and moved to the railing, peering down into the darkness below the deck.

"What is it?" Deborah joined her, wine glass in hand, her expression shifting from relaxed to concerned.

"Probably a raccoon." But even as she said it, she didn't believe it. Raccoons were lighter on their feet, and the sound had been too singular, too isolated.

"Did we make sure the garbage cans were closed?"

Deborah's practical nature kicked in, always looking for logical explanations.

That had to be it. "I'll go check." Shea set her glass on a round table and headed inside, grabbing a flashlight from the kitchen counter.

The lid to the trash can was firmly attached, secured with a bungee cord that looked like it hadn't been disturbed. Her gaze roamed the small clearing around the cabin, the flashlight beam cutting through the darkness. A deer froze in the light, its wide gaze meeting hers for a second before it bounded away with the distinctive white flash of its tail.

Shea smiled, shoving aside her paranoia. Of course, they weren't the only living things on that mountain. It was time to relax and enjoy the company of her friends. But even as she told herself this, she couldn't shake the feeling that something was watching them from the darkness beyond her flashlight's reach.

She made a complete circuit of the cabin, checking windows and doors, noting potential escape routes and defensive positions. Old habits died hard, and her training wouldn't let her enjoy the evening without ensuring their safety first.

When she returned to the deck, the conversation had turned to their college days, to memories of late-night study sessions and weekend adventures that seemed impossibly carefree in hindsight. Shea tried to join in, but part of her attention remained focused on the darkness beyond the deck lights, listening for sounds that didn't belong.

~

"Who's ready for a hike?" Becky sang out the next morning, her voice carrying the forced cheer of someone determined to make the best of things.

Shea groaned and pulled her sheet over her head. Her friend had always been a cheerful morning person, the type who woke up ready to conquer the world while everyone else needed an hour and several cups of coffee to function. "Coffee."

"Already brewed." Becky yanked off the sheet with the ruthless efficiency of a mother dealing with reluctant children. "Let's go, ladies. Eggs, bacon, and coffee wait on the deck. Plus, I've made sandwiches and got water bottles for the hike."

"Stop being a soccer mom for one weekend, Becky, and relax." Shea sat up, running her hands through her hair. Even here, surrounded by nature and away from all responsibilities, Becky couldn't turn off her caretaker instincts.

"I can't. It's who I am." She grinned and practically skipped from the room the two of them shared with Emma and Tessa. Her energy was infectious, but Shea suspected it was also a way of avoiding dealing with her marital problems.

"Is she going to be like that the whole time we're here?" Emma fell back onto her pillow, her usually perfect hair a tangled mess from sleep.

"Yep, so you'd better get up before she comes back

in." Shea pulled on a pair of short leggings, then donned the silly pink tee-shirt. They'd have to do a load of laundry if they were expected to wear the shirts every day.

She perked up a bit as she stepped onto the deck and grabbed a cup of coffee. The morning sun filtered through the trees, creating a dappled pattern on the wooden planks. Birds serenaded from the surrounding forest. A squirrel chattered from overhead, probably annoyed by their invasion of its territory. It was a wonderful morning for a hike.

The breakfast Becky had prepared was impressive—fluffy scrambled eggs, crispy bacon, fresh fruit, and homemade muffins that smelled like they'd come from a bakery. For someone who claimed to be falling apart, she was doing a fantastic job of holding things together.

Being assigned the leader by default due to her law enforcement background, Shea led the women away from the cabin after breakfast. A faint path headed down the bluff toward a creek that bubbled over rocks, the sound growing louder as they descended. She paused for a moment to study a set of footprints in the mud at the edge of the creek. Footprints that seemed fresh, the edges sharp and defined rather than worn smooth by weather.

The prints were large, definitely made by an adult, and they led both to and from the creek. Someone had been here recently, someone who hadn't bothered to stay on the established trail. She knelt down, examining the tread pattern, trying to determine what kind of boots had made the impressions.

She straightened and glanced around the area for sight of another cabin or someone camping. The forest stretched endlessly in all directions, dense and green and seemingly uninhabited. Not seeing anything obvious, the niggling of impending trouble returned, stronger now that she had concrete evidence they weren't alone.

"What are we waiting for?" Becky headed down the creek, her enthusiasm undimmed by Shea's cautious behavior. "I think there's a waterfall somewhere down here."

Shea sighed, took another glance around, then followed the rest of the group down the creek and into a clearing. The change from dense forest to open space was abrupt, as if someone had deliberately cleared the area. She caught up to them gathered around a large oak tree, their voices hushed and uncertain.

"Anyone know what that carving is?" Tessa pointed at a strange symbol cut into the bark, her expensive manicure stark against the rough tree trunk.

She moved closer, her law enforcement training kicking in as she studied the marking. It almost looked like a long-horned cow, but the horns were more demon-like than bovine, curved and sharp and somehow menacing. The carving was deep, deliberate, made with a sharp knife and considerable effort. "It looks like it's been here for a few years." The edges were weathered but still clearly defined, suggesting regular maintenance.

"Here's another one." Deborah pointed at a different tree, her voice tight with growing unease.

"And another." Rachel called out from across the clearing. "The carvings are on trees that form a circle."

As they spread out to examine the markings, the pattern became clear. Twelve trees formed a perfect circle around the clearing, each one bearing the same disturbing symbol. The precision was unmistakable—this wasn't random vandalism or teenage mischief. This was purposeful, ritualistic.

"Guys." Emma's voice shook as she stood in the center of the clearing. "This flat rock has a stain. Tell me that isn't blood."

Shea moved to the center of the clearing where a large, flat boulder sat precisely in the center of the circle of marked trees. A rust-colored stain covered the top and dripped down the sides in patterns that looked disturbingly like dried blood. She wanted to say hunters used the rock for processing game, but the words stuck in her throat. The stain was too extensive, too centrally located, and the surrounding area showed signs of regular use.

She knelt beside the rock, careful not to touch the stained surface. The boulder was naturally flat, almost like a table, and the stains followed channels carved into the stone—channels that hadn't occurred naturally.

This was definitely not a hunting site.

"What is it, Shea?" Annie stepped beside her, her voice barely above a whisper.

"I'm not sure, but it looks almost…cultish." The word felt strange in her mouth, but there was no other explanation that fit the evidence. The symbols, the circle of trees, the altar-like stone—it all pointed to some kind of ritualistic activity.

"Kids, maybe? Goofing around?" Annie's voice carried hope that this was all just elaborate pranks, but even she didn't sound convinced.

"Maybe." But she didn't think so. This level of organization, the precision of the carvings, the obvious care taken to maintain the site—this was the work of adults, and adults with a serious purpose. She'd heard stories of people hunting people, of modern-day cults that practiced rituals most people thought belonged only in horror movies. Everything in her wanted to head straight back to the van and leave this place immediately.

Instead, she took her cell phone out of her pocket and snapped photos from multiple angles, documenting the scene with the thoroughness of a crime scene investigation. The photos might be important later, especially if they needed to explain to local authorities what they'd found. "Anyone have service?"

"Haven't had service since we left the gas station," Rachel said, her pessimistic nature for once proving accurate. "This place gives me the creeps. Have you noticed how quiet this clearing is?"

It was true. The normal sounds of the forest—birds singing, insects buzzing, small animals moving through the underbrush—were completely absent here. Even the wind seemed to avoid the clearing, leaving it in an unnatural stillness that made every word they spoke seem too loud.

"We don't have service, so we're forced to unplug and relax." Becky's voice was determinedly cheerful, but Shea could see the fear in her eyes.

Shea had noticed the silence, and it added to her growing certainty that they needed to leave. "Let's move on." Back to where the shadows didn't seem as menacing. Next time they left the cabin, she'd make sure to wear her gun on her hip.

She hadn't thought they'd need it with ten women tramping through the woods. They made enough noise to scare away a bear. But they'd also made just enough noise to attract a predator that walked on two legs.

When they reached the small waterfall that poured over rocks, then over more rocks until reaching the creek they'd followed, Shea called a halt for lunch. Gone was the eeriness of the clearing, chased away once again by the sun through the trees and the singing of the water over stone.

Her friends chattered as they ate the sandwiches Becky had prepared, obviously having pushed the clearing from their minds, or at least trying to. Shea envied their ability to compartmentalize, to enjoy the beauty of their surroundings despite the ominous discovery. But she couldn't shake the images of those symbols, the stained stone, the unnatural silence.

She would find another way back to the cabin. One that didn't lead them back to where she'd felt evil as real as the faces of her friends.

"You're awfully quiet." Becky sat next to her on a fallen log, unwrapping her sandwich with careful precision. "Are you regretting our time away?"

"Of course not." The lie came easily, but she could see Becky wasn't convinced.

"You can't not be on edge, can you?" Her friend took a sip of water from her plastic water bottle. "You're always looking for trouble, even when we're supposed to be relaxing."

"Something doesn't feel right." Her instincts were rarely wrong, honed by years of experience and training. Out of the ten of them, she was the only one equipped to face people with dangerous intent, the only one who understood what they might be dealing with.

"Still thinking about those men at the gas station? I think they just wanted to intimidate us." Becky's voice carried the hope of someone trying to convince herself as much as anyone else.

"Maybe." But it was more than that now. The carvings on the trees were a warning; she felt it in her bones. Combined with the isolation, the lack of communication, and the obvious local knowledge that something was wrong with this place, they were sitting in the middle of a potential disaster.

She pushed to her feet, decision made. "Come on, girls. Let's get back to the cabin."

Words of agreement filled the air since they'd been walking for hours and now had to climb back up the embankment, which wouldn't be as easy as the trip down. The group began gathering their trash and water bottles, preparing for the return journey.

Shea stopped them halfway up the slope, spotting something through the trees that made her blood run cold. A flash of movement, too deliberate to be an animal, too far away to identify clearly. When she looked again, focusing intently on the spot, she saw nothing. But the feeling of being watched intensified, raising the hair on the back of her neck.

She continued to the top, breathing a sigh of relief at the sight of the road that would lead them back to the cabin. But the relief was temporary, replaced quickly by the realization of just how isolated they really were.

Usually, she was happy not to be crowded by other houses and people, but now the solitude of their cabin filled her with dread. Add in the fact that none of their phones were of any use, and they were in deep trouble if danger did come knocking.

She tried to shake off her dark feelings, but they'd hung over her since their first trip to the gas station. From when the attendant told her that no one came up here anymore. Intensified by the man in the ball cap's words and confirmed by the disturbing discovery in the clearing.

"You're making me nervous," Becky whispered as they walked. "You look like a cat ready to walk into a room full of German Shepherds."

Because that's exactly what she felt like. Rather than voice her concerns and potentially panic the group, she put an arm around her friend's shoulders. "I'm sorry. Just thinking. I know how much this week means to you."

"Good. Then brighten up. We're going to have the time of our lives."

Yes, but would it be a good time? Or would they be lucky to survive it?

Chapter Three

Shea grilled steaks on the deck grill, checking her phone for the umpteenth time in hopes of getting service. The screen showed the same frustrating message: "No Service." Thunder rumbled in the distance, a low, threatening growl that seemed to roll through the mountains like a warning. The thickening cloud cover didn't help with getting cell phone service, turning the sky an ominous gray-green that made the approaching evening feel more like twilight.

A few days away or not, she'd hoped to spend some time on her laptop learning more about the people she'd be working with. She'd brought files on the deputies who'd stayed when Westbrook retired, background information on recent cases, and departmental policies she needed to review. But without internet access, the laptop was useless for research, and her phone contained only the basic information Westbrook had provided during their brief conversations.

Stop moping about what couldn't be changed. She flipped the steaks one final time, the sizzling meat sending up clouds of savory smoke that mixed with the approaching storm's electric scent. She glanced upward, checking the darkening sky, and noticed the red light blinking on the security camera for the first time since their arrival.

Her blood went cold. The camera had been dark, lifeless, since they'd arrived. Now it pulsed with a steady red light that meant it was recording, transmitting, or both. She removed the steaks from the grill with hands that trembled slightly, turned off the gas with deliberate care, and carried the tray of meat into the house. As she entered, she glanced in every corner, her law enforcement training automatically cataloging what she saw.

Every camera now blinked red. Living room, kitchen, dining area—each one showing that telltale light that meant someone, somewhere, was watching them.

"Anyone have phone service?" She set the steaks on the kitchen counter, trying to keep her voice casual despite the adrenaline coursing through her system.

Gazes landed on phones throughout the room as each woman checked her device. Heads shook in unison, a chorus of disappointment and growing concern.

How were the cameras working? If there was no cell service, no internet, what powered these devices?

What allowed them to transmit data? The implications sent ice through her veins. Someone had deliberately set up a system that would work even when other communications failed.

Becky's gaze followed hers to the nearest camera. "Those weren't on before, were they?" Her voice carried the first hint of real worry, the cheerful mask she'd worn all day finally beginning to slip.

"No." Shea didn't like the fact they blinked now, didn't like the way the lights seemed to pulse in unison like synchronized heartbeats. She took the glass of wine offered by Melanie and stared at the camera as she took a sip, wondering who might be on the other end of that electronic eye.

The wine tasted sour in her mouth, and she realized she clenched her jaw tight enough to ache. She forced herself to relax, to appear calm for her friends' sake, but her mind raced through possibilities. Remote monitoring systems, battery-powered transmitters, satellite uplinks—all expensive, all requiring significant planning and technical knowledge.

There were enough cameras to show every inch of the cabin. The living areas, the kitchen, the dining room—every space where they might gather was under surveillance. She excused herself and moved to the bathroom, her suspicions confirmed when she found a camera there too, positioned to capture everything.

Even here. The violation of privacy was complete and deliberate. She took a washcloth off the shelf and covered the lens with deliberate movements. Whether there was someone on the other end of the camera or not, they wouldn't get a free show here. The thought of unseen eyes watching them shower, change clothes, or use the facilities made her stomach churn with disgust and anger.

When she returned to the main room, her friends looked at her with growing apprehension. Their earlier excitement about the weekend getaway was fading, replaced by the uncomfortable realization that something wasn't right about their supposed paradise.

Shea pasted on a smile, calling on years of experience dealing with frightened civilians. "Who wants to watch a sappy chick flick?" Unless she knew for sure trouble was coming, it was best not to worry the others. Panic would only make the situation worse, and she needed them calm and thinking clearly.

"Do you want me to drive down the mountain to look for a signal?" Becky whispered, moving closer so the others couldn't hear. Her face was pale, and Shea could see the questions in her eyes—questions about whether they were safe, whether they should leave.

"No. I'm probably just being paranoid." The lie felt heavy on her tongue, but she couldn't send Becky down that mountain alone. Not with those men from the gas station potentially watching the roads, not with the storm approaching. Two women were safer together than one alone.

"Paranoia isn't part of who you are." Becky sat on

the sofa, her movements careful and controlled. "I brought Steel Magnolias. The write-up on this place said it had Blu-ray."

"Sounds perfect." Shea moved to close the curtains, noticing they were motorized, controlled by a remote system. "These are on remote control. Where's the remote?" The windows offered too much visibility, making them too vulnerable to anyone watching from outside.

Becky shrugged, her expression troubled. "I couldn't find it. I looked everywhere when we first arrived."

Of course, she couldn't find it. Shea yanked the curtains closed manually on the three windows of the living and dining area, using the emergency cords hidden behind the fabric. The mechanical resistance told her the motor was fighting her efforts, but she was stronger than the machinery. Once the windows were covered, she chose a chair that gave her a good view of the front door and the one window she couldn't fully close.

The chair's placement was strategic, letting her watch the most likely entry points while her back was against a solid wall. Her friends might think she was just being social, but she was actually setting up a defensive position.

"What are you expecting to see come through that door?" Rachel asked, her voice carrying a nervous laugh that didn't reach her eyes. "That clearing we found today really rattled you, didn't it?"

"A bit. Looked like a sacrificial place." She took another sip of wine, hoping it would quell her nerves, though she knew she should probably stop drinking entirely. She needed her reflexes sharp, her thinking clear. She didn't want to spoil the time everyone had looked forward to, but she also couldn't ignore the growing evidence that they were in danger.

The ritualistic clearing, the watching cameras, the men at the gas station, the mysterious footprints—each element by itself might be explainable, but together they painted a picture she didn't like.

"Relax." Annie plopped onto the sofa, her blonde hair catching the lamplight. "We're the only people around for miles. It's what we wanted." But even as she said it, her voice lacked conviction, and she glanced nervously at the covered windows.

"I'm just anxious about my new job." Shea forced a smile, falling back on the partially true excuse. She was worried about the job, about proving herself in a new environment, but that concern paled in comparison to her growing certainty that they were being hunted.

"Don't be," Emma said, settling cross-legged on the carpet with characteristic flexibility. "You'll do great. Whoever gives you a hard time for being female is an idiot."

"Here, here!" the others said, lifting their glasses in a toast that felt forced but determined. "To Shea!"

Their confidence filled her with warmth despite the circumstances. These women had known her since college, had seen her at her best and worst, and they still believed in her. That faith meant everything, especially now when she was asking them to trust her instincts about danger they couldn't see.

"I really do have the best friends." She turned her attention to the television, determined to enjoy what might be their last peaceful moments together. The movie began, but she found it impossible to focus on the familiar story of friendship and loss.

Lightning flashed outside the window, illuminating the landscape for just a second. In that brief moment of stark white light, she saw what looked like the form of a man standing near the tree line, watching the cabin. The figure was there and gone so quickly she almost doubted what she'd seen.

Shea got slowly to her feet, moving with deliberate calm to avoid alarming her friends. She parted the curtains carefully, just enough to peer outside. Nothing. The darkness was complete, broken only by the occasional flash of lightning that revealed an empty yard and swaying trees.

Her imagination again? She wanted to believe that, but her training told her otherwise. The figure had been too solid, too still among the moving branches to be a trick of light and shadow.

She peered across the drive toward where they'd parked the van. The vehicle seemed to be sitting lopsided, but that could be a distortion through the now heavily falling rain. The weather was getting worse, the wind picking up and driving the precipitation sideways across the clearing.

She let the curtains fall back into place and headed to the bedroom she shared with three other women. Their luggage was scattered around the room, clothes and toiletries spread across surfaces in the casual chaos of a girls' weekend. She moved to the nightstand where she'd hidden her service weapon beneath a stack of paperback novels.

The gun felt reassuring in her hands, solid and familiar. She checked the chamber and the safety with automatic precision, then stuck the weapon in the waistband of her pants, pulling the ridiculous pink tee shirt low enough to cover the weapon before returning to her seat.

Imagination or not, she wouldn't be without her gun until the uneasiness plaguing her left. If she was wrong, she'd endure the teasing about her paranoia. If she was right, the weapon might save their lives.

A loud boom of thunder made her jump, the sound so close and violent it seemed to shake the entire cabin. She grinned at the others sheepishly, hoping they'd attribute her startle response to the weather rather than her heightened state of alert. "I love storms, but that one caught me by surprise."

"We ought to all sleep good tonight with the rain." Melanie moved to open a couple of windows, letting the sound of rainfall and the scent of ozone fill the room. The fresh air felt good, but it also made them more vulnerable to anyone approaching from outside.

Shea bit back the request for her to close them and forced her attention back to the movie. The familiar dialogue washed over her, but she found herself listening instead to the sounds from outside—the drum of rain on the roof, the whistle of wind through the trees, and underneath it all, the occasional sound that didn't belong.

Something clattered outside, a sharp metallic noise that cut through the storm sounds. She jumped to her feet and moved back to the front window, pushing the curtain aside again. The lid to the trash can blew across the lawn, tumbling end over end in the wind.

"There's going to be a mess to clean up unless I go out there." She eyed the downpour, calculating how long it would take to secure the garbage and whether the risk was worth it. "Don't pause the movie for me. I've seen it."

But really, she wanted an excuse to get outside, to check the perimeter, to see if her instincts about being watched were correct. She yanked open the front door and stepped onto the covered porch.

A strong wind pelted her with rain, despite the roof overhead; the storm drove the water sideways with enough force to soak her immediately. The drops were cold and sharp, plastering her hair to her neck and her shirt to her skin within seconds. Blinking against the onslaught, she retrieved the trashcan lid, fighting the wind that tried to tear it from her grasp.

She righted the overturned can, shoving back inside what garbage she could find scattered around the clearing. Most of it was soggy and disgusting, but leaving it out would only attract more attention—from animals or worse. She maneuvered the can between two trees, wedging it in place in hopes of keeping it from blowing over again. She looked for the bungee cord that had held the lid in place.

As she worked, she used the opportunity to scan their surroundings with the practiced eye of a law enforcement officer. The darkness was nearly complete, broken only by the cabin's exterior lights and the frequent lightning flashes that transformed the landscape into a stark black-and-white photograph.

She turned and studied the tree line more carefully, letting her eyes adjust to the darkness between lightning strikes. It seemed as if shadows moved among the trees, but it could be nothing more than the wind moving the thick brush. The rain made it hard to tell, creating visual noise that could hide almost anything.

A twig snapped from the side of the house, a sound distinct enough to cut through the storm noise. She whirled toward the sound, her hand instinctively reaching for her gun, body frozen in a defensive crouch. The sound had been close, too close, and too heavy to be a small animal.

When no other sound came, she tried to convince herself it was nothing more than a raccoon attracted by the blown-over garbage can. But raccoons didn't make sounds that heavy, that deliberate. And they certainly didn't move around in weather like this, did they?

Then why did the chill down her spine that had nothing to do with the rain continue? Something was very wrong. She'd never ignored her instincts before and shouldn't start now, especially not with nine other lives depending on her vigilance.

Everything in her wanted to tell the others to pack up and leave immediately, storm or no storm. But she knew they'd resist, would want explanations she couldn't provide without sounding paranoid or crazy. She needed more concrete evidence, or she needed the threat to become obvious enough that even civilians would recognize it.

She marched to the van, rain streaming down her face and soaking through her clothes. One tire was definitely flat, the vehicle listing to one side in a way that hadn't been apparent from the cabin windows. Upon closer inspection by lightning light, she located the nail—a long, thick construction nail that had been entirely driven through the tire.

The placement was too precise to be accidental. Someone had deliberately disabled their vehicle, trapping them on the mountain. The realization hit her like a physical blow, confirming her worst fears about their situation.

Nothing to do about it until morning, even if she wanted to attempt a repair in this weather. Hopefully, the rental had a spare tire and the necessary tools to change it, though she suspected whoever had sabotaged it wouldn't have overlooked such details.

"The van has a flat," she announced upon reentering the cabin, trying to keep her voice matter-of-fact despite the churning fear in her stomach. "We ran over a nail." The lie came easily, but she could see the questions in Becky's eyes.

Water dripped from her soaked clothes onto the cabin's hard wood floors, creating small puddles that reflected the lamplight. She headed to the bedroom to change out of her wet clothes and into the baggy shorts and oversized tee shirt she'd brought to sleep in.

The dry clothes felt good against her skin, but they also made her feel more vulnerable somehow. Pajamas weren't appropriate attire for facing whatever was coming, but she needed to maintain the pretense of normalcy for her friends' sake.

"Good idea." Tessa ran past her to change after spotting Shea in her bedclothes, apparently deciding that comfort was more important than fashion.

Soon, the others followed suit, transforming from a group of put-together women into something that looked more like an actual slumber party. They gathered around the television set again to finish the movie, but the easy camaraderie of earlier in the evening was strained now, replaced by nervous glances and forced laughter.

It didn't take long before all ten of them had tears streaming down their faces as the movie reached its emotional climax, wine glasses refilled for the third or fourth time since dinner.

This time, Shea only pretended to sip hers, tilting the glass to her lips but not drinking. If her gut was right about what might be coming, she would need all her wits about her. Alcohol would dull her reflexes, slow her thinking, and make her less effective when lives were on the line.

The storm outside showed no signs of stopping. If anything, it was getting worse, the wind howling around the cabin with increasing ferocity. The lights flickered ominously, the electrical system straining against the weather's assault.

The intermittent lighting spurred Becky to hunt for candles before they were all left in the dark. She returned from the kitchen cabinets with a collection of pillar candles and a lighter, setting them around the room in strategic locations. When the lights finally went out completely, plunging them into darkness broken only by the candles' dancing flames, she grinned with determined cheerfulness.

"How about ghost stories?" The suggestion carried an almost manic quality, as if Becky was trying too hard to maintain the illusion that this was still just a fun weekend getaway.

"This isn't a slumber party." Shea frowned, the idea of deliberately frightening her friends when real danger might be lurking outside striking her as particularly inappropriate.

"Sure, it is." Becky set another candle on the coffee table, the flame creating flickering shadows on the wall that seemed to move with lives of their own. "We're all in our pajamas, telling stories, drinking wine—what else would you call it?"

"Come on. It'll be fun. We're in the woods, without power, with a storm raging outside. How much spookier can it get?" Annie wrapped a crocheted blanket around her shoulders, suddenly looking much younger than her twenty-eight years. "I, for one, would like to hear something scary that's made up. Reality is frightening enough right now."

Becky sat down and hugged a pillow to her stomach, but Shea could see the tension in her shoulders, the way she kept glancing toward the windows despite the closed curtains.

A thud outside, followed by what sounded like a muffled shout. The sound cut through the storm noise with unmistakable clarity—that was a human voice, distorted by wind and rain but definitely human.

Shea moved to the window again, her heart rate spiking as she peered outside before pulling them closed. Lightning illuminated the yard in stark detail, showing her empty ground and swaying trees. But the voice had been real; she was certain of it.

"What do you expect to see?" Lauren exhaled heavily, her patience with Shea's vigilance finally wearing thin. "You're freaking us all out."

"I keep hearing things," Shea said over her

shoulder, not moving away from the window. Her eyes swept the visible area methodically, looking for any sign of movement, any indication that they weren't alone.

"Of course you do. It's storming outside and the wind is blowing." Lauren rested her head against the back of the chair she sat in, clearly exhausted by the tension that had been building all day.

"Do you remember why you went into law enforcement?" Rachel asked, her voice carrying the tone of someone trying to redirect a conversation that was getting too serious.

"Yes." Shea resumed her seat reluctantly, still listening to the sounds from outside. "Because I wanted to help people. Keep them safe." And wasn't that what she was doing now? Trying to protect her friends from a danger they couldn't see or understand?

"Also, because of Lindsey White. Remember her?" Rachel arched a brow, bringing up a memory from their college days. "You thought she'd gone missing. Been kidnapped, when what she'd really done was run off with that no-good boyfriend of hers."

The memory stung because it highlighted what her friends saw as a pattern of overreaction, of seeing danger where none existed. But they hadn't been there when she'd found evidence of struggle in Lindsey's dorm room, hadn't seen the broken lamp and overturned furniture that suggested something violent had occurred.

"Yeah, so?" Shea tried to keep the defensiveness out of her voice.

"You always think the worst of people." Rachel's words weren't meant to be cruel, but they hit their mark anyway.

"I do not." She scowled, but even as she said it, she wondered if they were right. Had years of law enforcement work made her paranoid, unable to enjoy simple pleasures without looking for threats?

"You do." Becky shrugged apologetically. "Ever since your father ran off, leaving you and your mother to fend for yourselves when you were ten, you expect people to hurt you. You've had a wall up ever since. I know because we've been friends since the first grade. We love you, Shea. Please don't take offense."

The psychological analysis was accurate and painful, striking at the heart of her deepest insecurities. Her father's abandonment had shaped her worldview, made her suspicious of people's motives, and quick to assume the worst about human nature.

True, she had trust issues, but that didn't mean she was wrong this time. Something evil was coming; she could feel it in her bones, in the way the air itself seemed charged with menace. "No offense taken." She cast another glance at the window, then forced her attention back to her friends. "Let's talk about something else. What do you want to do with the rest of our time? Hike again?"

"I enjoyed the hike," Annie said, apparently willing

to let the psychological discussion drop. "I'm up for that again, but let's go another way. Not through that clearing."

Even Annie, the most optimistic of their group, had been disturbed by what they'd found. That gave Shea some validation that her concerns weren't entirely unfounded.

"There is supposed to be a swimming hole around here somewhere," Becky said, consulting the notes she'd made when researching the area. "Let's try to find it tomorrow."

Conversation returned to how they'd spend the next few days, filling the hours with sleeping in, reminiscing, and exploring the woods. Becky suggested they find pinecones and interesting plants and make keepsake crafts, grasping for activities that would feel normal and safe.

"Plus, we need to take lots and lots of pictures, so you'll have to wear your T-shirts again. Just long enough for a photo," she added at the groans from around the room. "I forgot to take one today."

A gust of wind blew through the window Melanie had opened, bringing rain into the house and extinguishing one of the candles. Shea rushed to close it as another streak of lightning rippled across the night sky, illuminating the landscape in brilliant detail.

Something ran from behind the van, darting across the open ground and disappearing behind the trunk of a large tree. The movement was too quick, too purposeful to be a frightened animal. She narrowed her eyes, trying to see better through the rain-distorted glass, but the lightning faded and darkness returned.

She couldn't imagine wild animals out on a night like this, not moving with such deliberate intent. People either, for that matter, unless they had a very good reason to be skulking around in a storm. Whatever was out there, wild or not, was not friendly.

She no longer refused to believe they were alone on that mountain. The evidence was mounting, impossible to ignore or explain away. Tomorrow morning, she'd find a way to convince her friends they had to go, flat tire or no flat tire. Until then, she'd sleep with her gun under her pillow and pray that morning would come before whatever was hunting them decided to make its move.

"I know what we can play." She turned with what she hoped was a genuine smile, though she suspected it looked more like a grimace. "Everyone tell me what you brought in your bags. Don't leave anything out."

The request would seem like a harmless game to her friends, but really, she was conducting an inventory of potential weapons and resources. If they were going to face whatever was coming, she needed to know what they had to work with.

"I'll start." Becky tapped her forefinger against her teeth, thinking. "I brought food and water. An extra pair of shoes in case my feet get wet, keys to the van, an umbrella…my pillow…oh, and a pocketknife."

A pocketknife was better than nothing, though not much of a weapon against determined attackers. But it could be useful for cutting rope or breaking glass if they needed to escape.

"I brought pepper spray, keys, clothes, and my cell phone and wallet," Annie said. "That's about it. I packed light."

Pepper spray was good, effective at close range against one or two attackers. Annie's contribution to their defensive capabilities increased significantly in Shea's mental calculations.

"We know everyone brought clothes," Shea said, trying to keep the conversation moving. "Let's leave out the obvious." What she looked for was anything that could be used as a weapon or tool for escape.

"I have a Tazer," Emma added with a slight blush. "And cuticle scissors, lip stick, and pain reliever."

A Tazer was excellent, possibly their best weapon after the firearms. Emma had just become their most valuable team member in terms of self-defense capabilities.

Kara laughed. "I brought a book and a military-type knife. No one needs to ask whether Shea brought a gun or not. I saw it under her shirt earlier."

A military knife suggested serious cutting power, the kind of blade that could do real damage in the right hands.

"Ha, ha. I never go anywhere without it. Don't any of you carry a gun?" The question was probably too direct, but she needed to know their full defensive capabilities.

"I do." Becky raised her hand tentatively. "Wasn't sure I should make that public knowledge, though. Bill also said I should keep it a secret."

Two firearms, a Tazer, pepper spray, and at least two knives. They weren't helpless, but against multiple determined attackers, their chances would still be slim.

"Anyone else?" Shea glanced around the group, hoping for more weapons or at least useful tools.

"Why?" Tessa frowned, her voice carrying the first note of real alarm. "You really do think we're in trouble, don't you?"

The direct question hung in the air, demanding an honest answer. Shea could continue to pretend everything was fine, or she could start preparing her friends for what might be coming.

Shea shrugged, trying to appear casual despite the urgency she felt. "Something about this place doesn't feel right."

Becky jumped to her feet with sudden energy, moving with the purposeful efficiency that had made her such an effective mother and organizer. "Should we look for other weapons? I know Shea enough to know when she's overreacting. She isn't. I saw a filet knife in the kitchen. In the bedroom closet is a nail gun, a roll of some kind of wire, and a sawzall...I think that's what it's called."

Now they were getting somewhere. A nail gun

could be devastating at close range, and wire could be used for restraints or tripwires. The sawzall—a reciprocating saw—could cut through almost anything if they needed to make their own escape route.

"Gather anything that can be used as a weapon and put it on the kitchen table." Shea kept her smile in place despite her nerves vibrating like guitar strings. "I said we were playing a game, remember? This game is called survival."

Becky didn't look convinced as she headed for one of the bedrooms, but she followed instructions anyway. The expressions on the faces of the others softened somewhat, apparently buying into the game scenario rather than recognizing it as emergency preparation.

"Strange game," Rachel said as she moved to the kitchen, searching through drawers for potential weapons. "But you've always been a bit different, Shea."

The comment stung, but she ignored it in favor of watching her friends scatter through the cabin, gathering anything that might help them survive the night. Kitchen knives, fireplace tools, even heavy candlesticks—everything went onto the growing pile on the table.

A knock sounded on the front door, three measured raps that cut through the storm noise like gunshots.

Everyone froze, conversations dying mid-sentence, wine glasses halfway to lips. The sound was unmistakably human, unmistakably deliberate, and absolutely terrifying given their isolation and the late hour.

In the candlelit cabin, surrounded by the debris of their makeshift armory, nine pairs of eyes turned to Shea, looking for guidance from the only one among them trained to handle danger.

The knock came again, more insistent this time, and Shea's hand moved instinctively to the gun hidden beneath her shirt.

Chapter Four

Shea withdrew her weapon and put a finger to her lips, the familiar weight of the gun steadying her nerves even as her heart hammered against her ribs. "Becky, get your gun. The rest of you take down every security camera and destroy it."

The silence that followed was electric, charged with terror and disbelief. These women had come here for a relaxing weekend, not a fight for their lives. But reality had a way of forcing itself upon people, regardless of their expectations.

"We're renting this cabin," Rachel said, her voice barely above a whisper, wide eyes fixed on the front door as if it might explode inward at any moment.

"I'll take full responsibility. Go," Shea hissed, her law enforcement training taking over. Property damage was now the least of their concerns. Those cameras were how their attackers were watching them, coordinating their assault. Every lens that went dark was a tactical advantage.

The other women scrambled through the cabin like frightened animals, grabbing whatever they could reach to destroy the electronic eyes that had been watching them. The sound of breaking glass and splintering plastic filled the air as expensive surveillance equipment was reduced to debris.

Becky stood next to Shea, her hand shaking so violently that Shea thought her friend would drop the weapon before she could use it. The gun wavered in Becky's grip, and Shea could see the fear written across her face—not just fear of their attackers, but fear of the weapon itself, of what she might have to do with it.

Another knock sounded, louder than the one before, more insistent. The sound reverberated through the cabin like a death knell. Becky gasped, the sound sharp and painful in the tense atmosphere.

"We're isolated up here. I'm so sorry I didn't take your worries seriously." Becky's voice was thick with guilt and terror. "Maybe it isn't someone out to harm us. Maybe it's the landlord come to check on us."

Even as she said it, her voice carried no conviction. They both knew that no legitimate visitor would come calling at this hour, in this weather, to this isolated location.

"At ten p.m?" Shea shook her head, her eyes never leaving the door. "In a storm. After disabling our vehicle. No, Becky. This is what I was afraid of."

The confirmation of their worst fears hung between them like a physical presence. Everything Shea had sensed, all the warning signs she'd tried to rationalize away, had been leading to this moment.

"Oh, God," Becky whispered hoarsely, the reality of their situation finally sinking in completely. "What do we do?"

"Survive until morning, then get the heck out of here." Shea's heart almost stopped as the curtains started to open, the motorized system responding to someone outside with the remote control they'd never been able to find.

The implications hit her like a physical blow. Their attackers had complete control over the cabin's systems—lights, cameras, window coverings. They'd walked into a trap that had been carefully designed and prepared, possibly for years.

"Bedroom camera down." Melanie came down the hall, holding the remains of a surveillance device, her face flushed with the satisfaction of small rebellion. But as she stepped into the living room, a red dot appeared on her chest, bright as a laser pointer, steady as death.

Shea's blood turned to ice. "Get down!" she screamed, but it was too late.

Her eyes widened as she glanced at Shea, confusion replacing satisfaction. "What is that?"

A shot rang out, the sound deafening in the enclosed space. The bullet struck her heart with surgical precision, dropping her to the floor like a marionette with cut strings. The impact was immediate and final— no gasping, no last words, just the sudden absence of life from someone who had been vibrantly alive seconds before.

Annie screamed, a sound of pure animal terror that seemed to go on forever and dove out of sight behind the kitchen counter. The reality of their situation crystallized in that moment—this wasn't a robbery or a random attack. These men were killers, and they were playing with their victims like cats with mice.

Shea and Becky took cover behind the dining table, its solid wood construction offering some protection from the window. But they both knew it wouldn't stop a determined rifle round. They needed to cover the windows and block the sight lines that allowed their attackers to pick them off.

She needed to see to Melanie, needed to check for signs of life, even though she knew from her friend's sightless eyes that the wound was fatal. She couldn't do either without the risk of being shot. The sniper was still out there, still watching, still waiting for another target to present itself.

Then the curtains closed as suddenly as they'd opened, making it obvious who controlled the remote. Their attackers were demonstrating their power, showing the trapped women that every aspect of their environment was under hostile control.

She crawled to Melanie on hands and knees, keeping low, shouting for the others to cover the windows and barricade the doors. Her friend's body was still warm, but the pulse she felt for was absent, the wound too devastating for any chance of survival.

Looking into Melanie's eyes—eyes that just minutes ago had been bright with life and laughter—Shea felt something cold and hard settle in her chest. These men had just murdered one of the sweetest people she'd ever known, someone who wouldn't hurt a fly, someone whose biggest concern had been whether her students were learning enough in her third-grade classroom.

Scrambling to the bedroom, she yanked a quilt off the bed—a handmade piece with intricate stitching that spoke of love and care—and covered her friend's body. It seemed important somehow to afford Melanie that dignity, even in the midst of their desperate situation.

"Hurry. I don't know how long until they open the curtains again." Shea started hanging blankets over the bedroom windows, making sure they were locked. The glass wouldn't keep anyone out who was determined to get in, but at least it would slow them down and block the sight lines for their sniper.

Each lock she checked felt flimsy, inadequate against determined attackers. The windows were large, designed to showcase the beautiful mountain views, but now they were vulnerabilities that could be exploited by anyone wanting to gain entry.

Finished with one bedroom, she hurried to the door that led to the deck. The cliff beyond offered some protection—no one could enter that way unless they scaled the rock face, which seemed unlikely in this weather. Still, she covered the door with blankets and made sure the deadbolt was in place. Every precaution mattered now.

The blankets transformed the cabin from a bright, welcoming space into something that felt like a bunker, all dark corners and muffled sounds. But if it kept them alive until dawn, she'd gladly sacrifice the ambiance.

She returned to the living room to see the others trying to shove a heavy bookcase in front of the front door. Their movements were jittery and uncoordinated, driven more by panic than strategy. The bookcase was solid oak, probably weighing two hundred pounds, but adrenaline gave them the strength they didn't normally possess.

Laughter rang out on the other side of the door, cold and cruel and utterly without humor. Then someone spoke in a voice that carried easily through the wood. "Ready to play a game, ladies?"

The words sent ice through Shea's veins. This wasn't just about killing them—it was about terrorizing them first, drawing out their fear, making them suffer before the end. She'd heard about this kind of thing in law enforcement briefings, the kind of predators who hunted humans for sport.

"Don't answer." Shea put a finger to her lips again, fighting to keep her voice steady. "We don't want them knowing exactly where we are."

"Melanie?" Emma's eyes shimmered with unshed tears, her voice breaking on her friend's name.

"She's gone. We'll take time to mourn her later. Right now, we have to survive." The words came out harsher than Shea intended, but there was no time for grief, no luxury of processing their loss. They could fall apart later, if there were a later.

"We can't. I can't." Tessa's voice rose toward hysteria, the carefully controlled teacher facade cracking under the pressure. "I'm a teacher, not a soldier." She crumbled onto the sofa, her expensive braids falling across her face as she began to sob.

"You'll do what you have to." Shea's palm started to sweat around the handle of her gun, but her voice carried the authority she'd learned to project during crisis situations. "We all will."

Whoever these men were, they'd planned well. Shea and her friends weren't random targets—this felt personal, orchestrated, explicitly designed for them. The cabin was intended as a trap, every detail carefully arranged to ensure their victims would be isolated and helpless. No wonder no one had gone there in a very long time.

Why hadn't she heard about any deaths or attacks? People would've gone missing. Bodies would've been found...unless the bodies were never recovered. Her tongue turned to cotton as the implications sank in. How many others had walked into this same trap? How many families were still wondering what happened to their daughters, their sisters, their friends?

These men knew the cabin, the land, the woods.

They knew from the moment they spotted Becky and Shea at the gas station that the women would be isolated, trapped with no means of communication. The nail in the tire, the cameras, the remote-controlled curtains—it had all been planned in advance.

She stood in the center of the living room and studied every piece of furniture with new eyes. Pieces chosen for their beauty and comfort now needed to serve as the women's line of defense. The sofa, the bookcases, the heavy dining table—everything would have to be repurposed.

"Put the sofa on its end in front of that window. Take the mattresses from the beds and wedge them in front of the windows. Create the thickest barricade you can." She gestured toward the various pieces, her mind automatically calculating fields of fire and defensive positions.

The women moved with desperate efficiency, dragging furniture across hardwood floors that would probably never be the same. But property damage was irrelevant now—survival was the only thing that mattered.

"What about the attic?" Becky glanced toward the stairs, wiping sweat from her forehead despite the cool air. "There's a trap door at the top."

"I'll check it out. No one, under any circumstances, looks outside." She spared another glance at her fallen friend, her heart clenching at the sight of the quilt-covered form that had been laughing and teasing just hours before.

She climbed the stairs, each step creaking under her weight despite her attempts to creep. The attic access was a simple pull-down ladder, the kind found in thousands of homes across the country. When she pulled the rope, a set of wooden steps unfolded with a soft whisper of well-oiled hinges.

Taking a deep breath that tasted of dust and old wood, she climbed the steps. The attic held a lot of boxes, a chest, and a few pieces of furniture covered in white sheets like ghosts. At one end, a round window looked out over the deck, offering a view of the storm-lashed forest beyond.

Could the women get out that way? She tried to peer out to see whether there were footholds on the steep roof. The pitch was treacherous, especially in wet conditions, but if they wore shoes with good traction, they might be able to make it up and over. She'd spotted a trellis on one side of the house earlier that should be able to hold their weight. She hoped. It was a possibility anyway, better than being trapped inside like rats.

Hoping to find weapons or useful supplies, she dug through the boxes with increasing urgency. Baby clothes and toys mostly, tiny outfits that spoke of happy times and innocent dreams. A few photo albums showed a young family—mother, father, two small children—posing in front of the very cabin where she now crouched in fear.

A family had lived here once, had called this place

home. What had happened to them? Had they been hunted and toyed with as the women were now, or had they sold out, intending to return for their things someday? The boxes suggested the latter—people didn't abandon baby pictures and family heirlooms unless they intended to return.

But maybe they'd never gotten the chance. Maybe they'd become victims like Melanie, their stories adding to whatever sick collection their killers maintained.

When she returned downstairs, Tessa still lay curled in the fetal position on what remained of the sofa after they'd repositioned it, her sobs increasing in volume while the others stared at her with helplessness. The sound was grating, potentially loud enough to give away their exact positions to anyone listening outside.

Shea marched over to her and gripped her shoulders, giving her a shake that was firmer than she'd intended. "We need to stay focused. We'll get through this, but we can't lose control. All we have is each other."

Tessa's eyes were red and swollen, but she nodded and swiped a hand across her face. "Sorry. I'm sorry. I know I'm being useless."

"You're not useless. You're human. But right now, we need to channel that fear into action." Shea's voice softened slightly. "We're going to get out of this. I promise."

"Good. Everyone, grab a weapon. Keep it with you at all times." She gestured toward the pile of improvised weapons they'd assembled on the kitchen table—knives, fireplace tools, even heavy candlesticks that could serve as clubs.

"Then what?" Emma picked up the filet knife, testing its weight and balance. "I don't know if I can actually...you know."

"If your life depends on it, you can." Shea's voice carried absolute certainty. "When it comes down to survival, you'll discover strength you didn't know you had."

As time passed, the air in the cabin grew stifling despite the storm raging outside. The combination of fear, adrenaline, and blocked ventilation was taking its toll. The low-burning candles did little to dispel the oppressive atmosphere of terror hanging over them all.

The women gathered in the center of the room, backs together like wagons in a circle against attacking Apache. It was a defensive formation as old as human conflict, born from the instinctive knowledge that unity was their only hope against superior numbers.

Footsteps paced back and forth on the front porch, each footfall loud and deliberate as if the person there wanted to let the women know exactly where he was. The sound was maddening in its regularity, a psychological weapon designed to fray their nerves and maintain constant pressure.

Shea raised her gun and tried to determine which way he paced, counting steps, timing the pattern. Maybe she could even the odds a bit by taking one of them down. Every attacker eliminated improved their chances of survival.

"Anything in the attic that will help us?" Rachel asked, her voice barely above a whisper.

"A possible way out once it's light outside. We'll have to go one at a time over the roof and down the trellis." The escape route wasn't ideal, but it was better than being trapped inside indefinitely.

"No way." Emma shook her head vigorously. "You go and get help. Leave us here."

"We stay together." At least for now. There might come a time when someone would have to venture out, but she wasn't ready to abandon any of her friends. "I'm going to the deck. Maybe there's a way out that doesn't require scaling the cliff."

"You'll be shot." Deborah reached for her, genuine concern replacing the earlier irritation with Shea's vigilance.

"Those men seem focused on the front for now. I'll be careful." She had to know one way or the other if they could flee come daylight. Information was power, and right now they had too little of both.

She grabbed the military-grade knife she'd set on the table when they'd all gathered weapons and shoved it in her pocket. The blade was serious business—sharp enough to cut through rope or clothing, heavy enough to do real damage in close combat. If she saw the opportunity to take out one of their attackers, she'd need a knife. A gun would alert his buddies and bring them all running.

"Be careful." Becky blinked rapidly as if trying not to cry, her earlier composure finally cracking. "We won't survive without you."

"You're stronger than you think. All of you." Shea drew a breath sharply through her nose, steeling herself for what she had to do, then headed for the back door, stopping to change out of the pink tee-shirt that would make her visible from a mile away and into a black one that would help her blend with the shadows.

After pulling back the blanket and peering out for several minutes, studying the deck and the surrounding area for signs of movement, Shea slowly unlocked the sliding glass door. The sound seemed impossibly loud in the silence, but the storm provided cover for small noises.

Moving as slowly and quietly as possible, she slid the door open just enough to squeeze through and stepped onto the deck. The wind hit her immediately, driving rain against her face and soaking through her clothes within seconds.

The aroma of the grilled steaks they'd had for supper still lingered in the air, a surreal reminder of how normal their evening had started. Just hours ago, they'd been laughing and talking about old times. Now one of them was dead, and the rest were fighting for their lives.

She took another peek over the back railing, confirming what she'd suspected earlier. Absolutely no way down without climbing gear. The cliff face was nearly vertical, offering no handholds or footholds that would support a human being. Anyone trying to descend that way would fall to their death on the rocks below.

The left side of the deck had less of an embankment beneath it. She might be able to jump, but the drop was still twenty feet at least, enough to break bones, and she wouldn't have a way back up even if she survived the fall. Abandoning her friends wasn't an option anyway.

The right side showed more promise. She studied the tree branch hanging over the deck, estimating distances and angles. If she could get up there, she could scale the tree and drop to the ground. The lowest branch was maybe five feet above ground level once she was down—she'd need something to stand on in order to get back up.

She smiled grimly, spotting a sawed stump that had been used for chopping wood. The axe wasn't in the stump, but it was hopefully nearby. It would provide them with another effective weapon. An axe could stop an attacker permanently with a single well-placed blow.

Using one of the deck chairs, she climbed onto the branch hanging over the deck and belly-crawled toward the trunk. The rough bark scraped her stomach through her thin shirt, and she had to bite her lip to keep from making noise. From her elevated position, she could see ball cap guy occasionally stroll into sight as he continued his maddening pace around the front of the cabin.

She'd have to time her descent carefully, waiting for him to move away from her position. Getting caught in the open would mean certain death, and her friends needed her alive.

She froze as a man with a scraggly gray beard came around the corner of the house, moving with the casual confidence of someone who believed he was in complete control. He stopped and relieved himself on a rose bush, marking his territory like an animal, then returned out of sight.

The casual nature of the act was almost more terrifying than direct threats. It showed how confident these men were, how certain they were of the outcome. To them, this was just entertainment —a game with a predetermined outcome.

Shea heaved a sigh of relief when he disappeared, then dropped with a thud to the ground. The impact reverberated through her body, jarring her teeth and sending sharp pain through her ankles. She ducked behind the thick tree trunk to catch her breath and listen for any indication that she'd been heard.

"Ladies," someone called out in a sing-song voice that made her skin crawl. "Why not come out? We'll let you have a running start. It'll be fun. We'll be kind enough to give you a half-hour head start."

The men wanted to hunt them like animals, to chase them through the forest in the dark and the rain.

The idea was so monstrous that Shea's hand tightened on the knife handle until her knuckles went white. These weren't just killers—they were sadists who derived pleasure from their victims' terror.

She pulled the knife from her pocket and flipped it open, the blade locking into place with a soft click. The metal felt cold and solid in her hand, a tool of survival in a situation where violence was a necessary means to survival.

"Pssst."

She glanced up to see Becky peering over the rail, her face pale in the dim light from the cabin. Shea frowned and waved her back, not wanting her friend to become a target.

"Catch this." Becky tossed something down, then ducked out of sight like a prairie dog retreating into its burrow.

The pink Tazer lay in a pile of pine needles, looking almost festive against the dark forest floor. After a quick glance to make sure no one would see, Shea grabbed it, checking to make sure it was armed and ready. The device was small but effective at close range—it could drop a man instantly if she could get close enough to use it.

She plastered her back against the tree trunk again, her mind racing through tactical possibilities. She could do this. She had weapons, the element of surprise, and motivation stronger than her attackers could imagine.

She jumped out from behind the tree and moved

the stump close enough for her to reach the branch when she needed to get back up. Then she ducked behind a bush to wait for a chance to make her next move. Where was the axe? She needed that weapon if she was going to have any real chance of success.

Ball Cap had stopped his pacing from what she could tell, which made him more dangerous. A stationary target was easier to predict, but a stationary guard was also more likely to spot movement in his vicinity.

Every few minutes, he would call out to the women inside, taunting them with promises of a quick death if they surrendered or extended torture if they continued to resist. Each taunt was designed to increase their fear, to break down their will to fight.

Leaves rustled behind Shea, too close and too deliberate to be caused by wind. She whirled around, adrenaline spiking, to see a man with the axe she'd been seeking. He was large, bearded, and wearing camouflage that helped him blend with the forest shadows.

Without hesitation, she thrust out the Tazer, pressing it against his chest and triggering the electrical charge. The man fell instantly, his body convulsing as fifty thousand volts disrupted his nervous system. The axe clattered to the ground beside him.

Moving quickly while he was incapacitated, Shea grabbed the axe from his twitching hand and buried the blade into his chest with all the strength she could muster. The impact was sickeningly solid, the blade biting deep into bone and tissue. The man's eyes went wide for a moment, then vacant.

She'd killed a man. The reality of it hit her like a physical blow, but there was no time for hesitation or regret. This was war now, and war had different rules than civilized society.

Making a mad dash for the stump, she planted one foot on the wooden surface and propelled herself up into the tree, returning to the deck the same way she'd left. The man's buddies would come looking for him soon, and if they found her on the ground, they'd kill her or worse—force her to play some sordid game that would end with her death anyway.

Once back inside the cabin, she locked the door and plastered her back to the wall to catch her breath. Her heart was hammering so hard she could hear it in her ears, and her hands were shaking from adrenaline and the aftershock of taking a life.

"Why are you covered in blood?" Kara stepped from the bathroom, her eyes widening as she took in Shea's appearance.

"I killed one of them." Shea peeled off the soiled T-shirt, looking at the dark stains with a mixture of revulsion and grim satisfaction. One down, however many left to go.

She headed for the bathroom to wash the blood from her hands and arms, the warm water turning pink as it swirled down the drain. The metallic smell of blood filled her nostrils, but she forced herself to focus on the practical need to clean up.

Kara followed her into the small space. "I think I can squeeze through that window."

Shea eyed the petite woman, noting her small frame and agile build. "And then what?"

Kara had always been the athlete of their group, the one who ran marathons and climbed mountains for fun. If anyone could make it through the forest to get help, it would be her.

Hitching her chin with determination, she said, "I'll make my way to the gas station or wherever I can get cell phone service and call for help."

"What if you don't make it?" The question was brutal but necessary. They had to consider all possibilities.

"Then at least I'll have tried. Someone has to take the chance."

Cursing erupted from the side of the cabin, loud and violent, and getting closer. Someone had found their dead friend, and they weren't happy about it.

Shouts of revenge followed, promising graphic violence and slow death for whoever had killed their companion. The threats were detailed and creative, leaving no doubt about the attackers' intentions.

"It'll be more dangerous now." Shea wanted to tell her to stay, to keep their group together, but she knew it might be their only chance to call for help before the situation deteriorated further.

"I can do this. I'm fast and small." Kara nodded, psyching herself up for what might be a suicide mission. "Yes. I can do this."

74

Chapter Five

Shea stared for a long moment at Kara, studying her petite frame and the determined set of her jaw. The decision to send someone out into the night was agonizing, but staying trapped in the cabin meant slow death for all of them. At least this way, one of them might survive to tell their story.

Then she nodded. "Let me tell the others." She headed to the living room, her bare feet silent on the hardwood floors. "Give Kara the filet knife. She's going to make a run for help."

The announcement hit the group like a physical blow. Emma's face went white, and Annie started to protest before catching herself. They all understood the implications—Kara might be walking to her death, but she was also their only hope.

"Why don't we all run?" Tessa glanced around the group with wild eyes, her teacher's composure completely shattered. "If she can, we can, right?"

"We won't all fit through the bathroom window."

Shea shook her head, trying to project more confidence than she felt. "Nor can we risk us all going down the tree. We'd be caught for sure. Our best bet is to stick it out until help comes."

The logic was sound, but that didn't make it any easier to accept. Splitting up went against every survival instinct, but sometimes the right choice was also the hardest choice.

"Help that's too late for Melanie." Emma slouched in a chair.

Tessa handed Shea the knife with trembling fingers. The blade felt heavier than it should have, weighted with the responsibility of potentially saving or ending a life. The women followed her to the bathroom where Kara stood on the toilet lid, testing the window's size and checking the distance to the ground below.

"It's kind of high," Kara said, measuring the drop with her eyes. The window was at least eight feet off the ground, enough to cause injury if she landed wrong.

"I'll lift you down. Get on your belly, feet first through the window, and I'll grab your hands." Shea's voice was steady despite the churning in her stomach. When Kara positioned herself as instructed, Shea took her place on the toilet lid. "Don't die, okay?"

The words were inadequate, carrying the weight of everything she couldn't say—how much their friendship meant, how proud she was of Kara's courage, how desperately she hoped they'd see each other again.

Kara gave a shaky laugh that didn't quite mask her

terror. "I'm hoping not to. If help doesn't come in two days…well."

"Don't think that way. Even if it takes longer." God, don't let it take longer. Shea could act optimistic, but she knew her resolve would fade with each passing day. The psychological pressure of their situation was already wearing on all of them, and time was not their ally.

She gripped Kara's wrists, feeling the rapid pulse beneath her fingertips, and lowered her out the window as far as she could reach. The position was awkward, straining her shoulders and back, but she held on until Kara was as close to the ground as possible.

Her friend landed with a crunch in a bed of dry leaves but immediately gave a thumbs up, rolling to absorb the impact like the athlete she was. The sound seemed impossibly loud in the quiet night, and Shea held her breath waiting for shouts or gunfire.

"Make haste. Stay to the trees," Shea whispered, slowly closing the window and trying not to think about whether she'd ever see her friend alive again.

Kara nodded and raced for the tree line with the fluid grace of someone who'd spent years running trails and climbing mountains. When no shots or shouts rang out, Shea released the breath she'd been holding. Kara might make it. She was small and fast, just as she'd said, and within seconds she'd melted into the shadows like a ghost.

But even as relief flooded through her, Shea knew

the most challenging part was just beginning. Now they had to wait, trapped in their makeshift fortress, wondering if their friend would reach safety or become another victim of the predators stalking them.

A thud sounded on the front door, then another and another. The impacts were rhythmic, deliberate, like someone beating out a funeral dirge. Were the men throwing rocks at them? The psychological warfare was escalating, designed to fray their nerves and break down their will to resist.

A few seconds later, country music blared from multiple sources, the volume cranked high enough to vibrate the cabin's windows. The sudden assault of sound made everyone jump, their already frayed nerves sparked to new levels of tension.

Shea hurried to the front window and peered through a gap in their barricade. Four trucks sat in their driveway like mechanical beasts, headlights blazing directly at the house, doors open, all tuned to the same radio station. The positioning was deliberate—the lights would destroy their night vision, making it impossible to see into the darkness beyond.

The men were using psychological warfare, trying to break them down mentally before moving in for the kill. It was a tactic used by military forces and terrorists alike, designed to exhaust their targets and make them more compliant.

"Get some rest if you can." She sat in a kitchen chair facing the front door, her weapon ready and her eyes scanning for any sign of movement. "This could go on for a while."

"I've got earplugs." Becky rushed to the bedroom and returned with a small bag of purple foam plugs. "Just in case someone snored." She gave a sheepish grin, trying to inject some normalcy into their nightmare situation.

"You think of everything." Shea smiled despite their circumstances. Becky's preparedness had probably saved their lives multiple times already tonight. If only one of them could think of a way out of their current situation that didn't involve waiting for rescue that might never come.

As rocks continued to be thrown, music blared at deafening volumes, and heavy footsteps pounded on the front porch in a deliberate show of intimidation, Shea thought long and hard about their tactical situation. The other women, seemingly secure that she would keep guard, had gone to lie down in the bedrooms. Good. They would need their strength for whatever was coming.

The psychological assault continued for hours, a relentless barrage designed to prevent sleep and increase stress. Shea found herself jumping at every new sound, her nervous system pushed to the breaking point by the constant stimulation. She understood now why this was considered torture—the inability to relax or rest was wearing her down faster than physical violence would have.

Shea closed her eyes, trying to get some rest despite the constant noise outside. Her body was exhausted, running on adrenaline and caffeine, but her mind refused to shut down. Every creak of the cabin, every shift in the wind, every change in the music's tempo had her instantly alert and ready for action.

When the music stopped abruptly, her eyes snapped open. The silence screamed louder than the music had, filled with ominous potential. Sudden quiet meant their attackers were planning something new, something that required stealth.

She got to her feet and peered outside, careful to stay hidden behind the barricade. One armed man stood guard near the trucks, his rifle held ready across his chest. Six others sat inside the trucks or in the truck beds, their forms barely visible in the darkness. So, they'd decided to sleep, too, confident enough in their position to rest in shifts.

She eyed the lone awake guard, her tactical mind automatically calculating angles and opportunities. It wouldn't be hard to lure him away from the group and take their number down to six. Every enemy eliminated improved their odds significantly.

Biting her lip, she watched as he lit a cigarette, the flame from his lighter briefly illuminating a face scarred by violence and hard living. The red glow as he took a drag revealed a crooked nose and cold eyes before fading back into darkness. This was Ball Cap, the man she'd identified as their leader, though he was currently dozing in the front seat of an older model Chevy.

The body of the man she'd killed earlier had been laid on the front porch like a grisly trophy, a reminder of what she was capable of and a warning to the others. The sight should have made her sick, but instead she felt only grim satisfaction. One down, however many left to go.

There would be no getting out through the front door—not with a body blocking the way and armed men watching every movement. She'd have to climb down the tree again, risk another confrontation in the darkness. The thought of killing again left her nauseous, conflicting with everything she'd been trained to believe about law enforcement.

Her job was to serve and protect, not turn into a merciless killer. But these weren't ordinary criminals— they were predators who hunted human beings for sport, and they'd already murdered one of her closest friends. Sometimes protecting innocent people required terrible choices.

With all but one man asleep, it was now or never. Every minute of delay was another minute Kara might need to reach safety and call for help.

She headed out back again, moving with the careful precision of someone who understood that a single mistake would mean death. The tree felt familiar now, almost like an old friend, and she scaled it with practiced efficiency. She landed with ease on the stump she'd positioned earlier, freezing to listen for any sound that might indicate she'd been detected.

The forest was alive with small sounds—wind through branches, the distant call of an owl, the rustle of small animals moving through underbrush. All normal, all reassuring in their mundane nature.

She moved carefully to the ground, every sense hyperalert for danger.

"Hello, Darlin'."

The voice came from directly behind her, causing her heart to nearly stop. She whirled to see a man in a sleeveless flannel shirt step from under the deck, where he'd apparently been waiting for her return. He was large, muscular, with the kind of casual confidence that came from years of violence.

"We wondered how you got out to kill Dave." He grinned, revealing teeth stained by tobacco and poor hygiene. "Clever girl."

The tone was almost admiring, as if he respected her tactical thinking even as he prepared to kill her. These men saw murder as a game, and she'd proven herself a worthy opponent rather than easy prey.

Shea gripped her knife tighter, feeling the familiar weight of the weapon in her hand. "I'm Sheriff Callahan. You men will not get away with this."

Even as she said it, she knew how futile the words were. But sometimes maintaining your identity—remembering who you were beneath the violence—was the only thing that kept you human.

"Oh, I think we will." He took a step forward, his movements predatory and confident. "See, this isn't the first time. It is the first for such a large group, though. Makes it more of a challenge. More fun. The boss, Darryl, will be glad to know we've got ourselves law enforcement. Put down that knife, and I won't kill you."

"Yet." She wasn't stupid. They'd most likely kill her slowly and loudly to draw the other women out of the cabin, use her screams as psychological warfare against her friends. She lunged forward without warning, hoping to catch him off guard.

Sleeveless dodged her initial stab, his grin widening as he pulled a knife from his belt. The blade was longer than hers, serrated along one edge, designed for maximum damage rather than precision. "This is going to be fun."

Shea's heart pounded, and her hand started to sweat despite the chill of the night air. Adrenaline burned through her veins like liquid fire, sharpening her senses and making time seem to slow. Gaze steady on the man facing her, she prepared herself mentally for hand-to-hand combat, calling on years of training and natural instinct.

Use the knife as an extension of her hand. Jab like she was in her kickboxing training. Stay mobile, don't let him pin her down, or use his superior size and strength against her.

The man's first swipe went wild, overconfident and poorly aimed. Shea dodged easily, feeling the blade slice through the fabric of her shirt without touching skin. She backed up, finding her footing on the dry leaves crunching underfoot, using the uneven terrain to her advantage.

The man's teeth bared in a feral snarl, and he growled low in his throat as he came at her again. This time, his attack was more controlled, the blade moving in tight arcs designed to corner her against the cabin wall.

Shea raised her arm, deflecting his strike with the back of her forearm. Pain shot through her arm like electricity, but the wound wasn't deep—not yet. It wasn't her knife arm, and the injury only served to fuel her determination. The man might be stronger, but Shea was fueled by a desperate desire to save her life and the lives of her friends.

She gave him a roundhouse kick to the ribs, putting all her weight behind it. The impact was solid, driving the air from his lungs in a whoosh and causing him to stumble backward. The opening was exactly what she needed.

She leaped forward, grabbing his wrist and twisting it behind him with a move she'd practiced hundreds of times in training. The leverage forced him to drop his knife, the weapon clattering to the ground among the fallen leaves.

But he was experienced in violence, and he threw his head back hard, catching her on the chin with the back of his skull. Stars exploded across her vision, and she stumbled backward, losing her balance and her grip on his arm.

He dove for the dropped knife, his fingers scrambling through the leaf litter. She kicked it away, sending it spinning into a pile of debris where it disappeared from sight. Before he could react, she jumped on his back, grabbing him by the collar and using his momentum to slam him into the nearest tree.

His head hit the trunk with a sickening thud that seemed to echo through the forest. He stepped back, visibly dazed, his eyes losing focus for a crucial moment. But he was tough, tougher than she'd hoped, and he shook off the impact faster than she'd expected.

He threw a wild punch that caught her squarely in the jaw, snapping her head back and filling her mouth with the metallic taste of blood. She staggered against the cabin wall, her vision blurring as pain exploded through her skull.

The man charged again, trying to tackle her while she was stunned. It was precisely the wrong move—Shea used his momentum against him, stepping aside at the last second and raising her knife. Physics did the rest.

He impaled himself on the blade, his own weight and speed driving the steel deep into his abdomen. They both went down hard, Shea rolling until she straddled him, pushing the knife deeper to ensure he couldn't continue fighting.

"I'm sorry, but you gave me no choice." She looked

into his eyes as the life faded from them, feeling obligated to acknowledge the humanity she was ending, even as she knew it was necessary for survival. She sighed as his gaze went glassy and unfocused, then got shakily to her feet.

Two men dead by her hand in one night. The weight of it settled on her shoulders like a lead blanket, but there was no time for guilt or regret. Her friends were counting on her, and Kara was somewhere out there in the darkness, racing toward help that might arrive too late.

Not waiting to see whether the sounds of their struggle had reached the guard out front, she dashed for the tree stump and swung herself into the familiar branches. Her body was getting used to the route, muscle memory making the climb easier despite her exhaustion and injuries.

As soon as her feet hit the deck, Becky opened the back door. Her friend's face was streaked with tears, eyes wide with fear and relief in equal measure.

"Don't leave again without telling me." Tears poured down her face as if a dam had burst. "I thought something had happened to you." Her gaze fell on Shea's bleeding arm. "You're injured. Tell me you took down another one."

"I took down another one." She brushed past her friend, needing the comfort of walls around her, the illusion of safety that the cabin provided. "I saw an opportunity and took it."

The admission felt like a confession, as if she was acknowledging her transformation from protector to predator. But survival sometimes required becoming something you never thought you could be.

"Come into the bathroom and let me tend to that cut." Becky wiped her arm across her eyes and led the way, falling back into her caretaker role as a way of coping with their nightmare situation. "Sit." She pointed to the toilet. "We won't survive without you, Shea. You can't take risks like that."

"There might come a time when we all have to take risks." She removed the bloody, torn T-shirt, adding it to the growing collection of ruined clothes. At this rate, she'd have nothing to wear except for the ridiculous pink shirt.

"Did you see Kara?" Becky's hands were gentle as she cleaned the knife wound, her nursing instincts taking over despite her lack of formal medical training.

"No." And that was good—it meant Kara had made it into the forest without being detected.

"That's good, right?" Becky's voice carried desperate hope, the need to believe that something was going their way.

Shea nodded, then hissed as her friend poured antiseptic over the wound. The burn was immediate and intense, but necessary to prevent infection. "Does it need stitches?"

"I think so, but butterfly Band-Aids should work well enough if you don't mind a scar." Becky worked with careful precision, pulling the edges of the wound together before applying the adhesive strips.

Shea gave a short laugh that held no humor. "A scar is the least of my worries. How long until Bill sends out an alarm when he doesn't hear from you?"

"He won't try to contact me. I told him I needed time away and not to call unless something happens to one of the boys. I don't know about the others." Becky's voice caught as she realized the implications—no one would miss them for days, possibly weeks.

Pounding resumed on the front door, more violent this time, as if someone was using a sledgehammer. "I want to talk to whichever one of you is killing my men!"

The voice was different from before—deeper, more authoritative. This had to be Darryl, the leader she'd heard about.

"That would be me." Shea got to her feet, adrenaline spiking at the direct challenge.

"He can wait." Becky motioned her back down, continuing her medical work with determined focus. "That cut needs one more Band-Aid. It took four." She placed the last adhesive strip with careful precision. "Now, you can go."

Shea moved to the front door, her voice carrying clearly through the wood. "What's the matter, Darryl? Can't handle the game turning in your direction?"

"Who are you?" The question carried genuine curiosity along with respect for an opponent who'd proven more dangerous than expected.

"Sheriff Callahan of Steele County." She let authority ring in her voice, the badge giving her strength even when everything else seemed hopeless.

"You ex-military?" There was something in his tone that suggested he recognized professional training when he encountered it.

No, but she wouldn't tell him that. Let him worry about what kind of opposition he was facing. "You know all you need to know about me except for one thing."

"What's that?"

"You aren't going to win at this game." The words were a promise and a threat rolled into one.

"We'll see about that." Footsteps receded, but Shea could hear him talking to his men, probably planning their next assault.

Instinct had her moving away from the door, years of training screaming warnings about what was coming. "Get down, Becky."

They took shelter behind the couch as gunfire erupted, the sound deafening in the enclosed space. Automatic weapons shattered windows and pummeled the door, bullets chewing through wood and glass like termites through timber. The men had escalated to full warfare, abandoning any pretense of cat-and-mouse games.

Still, the log cabin should withstand the assault. The original builders had constructed it to last, with thick walls and solid foundations. The bookcase and mattresses they'd used as barricades took the brunt of the attack, absorbing bullets that would otherwise have filled the room with deadly projectiles.

By the time the gunfire ceased, the others had joined them in the living room, all looking shaken but unharmed. The sudden silence was almost as jarring as the violence had been.

"I think I preferred the country music." Rachel headed for the kitchen, her hands shaking as she reached for the coffee pot. "I'm making coffee. We need some normalcy."

"How about omelets?" Becky joined her, falling back on domestic routines as an anchor in their chaos. "We need to keep our strength up."

If brewing coffee and cooking kept her friends calm and functional, then Shea was all for it. She sat on the sofa and put her head back, feeling the exhaustion settle into her bones like lead. She needed sleep more than anything else, but rest seemed impossible with death lurking just outside their door.

"You went out again." Tessa's statement was flat, matter-of-fact, but Shea could hear the accusation beneath it.

"I did." She closed her eyes, trying to find some peace in the darkness behind her eyelids. "They are now down two. That leaves six. I like those numbers better."

The mathematics of survival were brutal but

necessary. Every enemy eliminated improved their odds, brought them closer to seeing morning alive.

"Would someone get my inhaler out of my bag, please?" The exertion of the fight had her lungs squeaking like an old screen door, the stress triggering her asthma worse than any allergen ever had.

"I want out. I want to go after Kara. She might need me." Tessa started pacing, her movements becoming more agitated with each step. "Really no one should be alone. You said it yourself. We should all stick together. Yes. I should go."

Shea opened her eyes, recognizing the signs of an impending panic attack in her friend's rambling speech and increasingly frantic movements. Fear had taken control, threatening to override rational thought.

"No." She got to her feet and gripped Tessa's shoulders, forcing eye contact. "Look at me. I'm covered in blood and wounded. I'm trained for this, you aren't." She smiled her thanks to Deborah, who handed her the inhaler, and took two measured puffs.

"I can fight. I'll take Becky's gun." Tessa's voice was rising toward hysteria, the teacher's usual calm completely shattered.

"No, you won't," Becky called from the kitchen, her tone brooking no argument. "I love you, but my gun stays with me."

"The subject is closed, Tessa." Shea led her to a kitchen chair, using the same firm but gentle tone she'd use with a frightened civilian at a crime scene. "Sit and have a cup of coffee."

The music started outside again as the sun began to rise over the mountain, painting the sky in shades of pink and gold that seemed out of place given their circumstances. Shea had managed to grab a couple of hours of sleep, but it wasn't enough. Not nearly enough. Her body was running on fumes, adrenaline, and caffeine.

She poured her second cup of coffee, taking it black despite her usual preference for cream and sugar. She winced at the bitter taste but needed the caffeine more than she needed the drink to be palatable.

"Kara has been gone for hours." Rachel plopped on the sofa, exhaustion written in every line of her body. "Do you think she made it?"

Shea nodded, trying to project more confidence than she felt. "I think Darryl out there would've bragged if they'd caught her. They have no idea one of us is gone." Her gaze flicked involuntarily to where Melanie's body lay beneath the quilt. Two actually, though only one by choice.

She wanted to keep it that way. Their enemies' ignorance was one of the few advantages they had left, and she intended to protect it as fiercely as she protected her friends' lives.

Chapter Six

Tessa continued her pacing and mumbling, wearing a path in the hardwood floor like a caged animal. Every once in a while, Shea could make out the words, "We need to leave." Her friend chanted them like a mantra, twisting her hands as she went back and forth, her movements becoming more agitated with each repetition.

The sight was heartbreaking. Tessa had always been the composed one, the teacher who could handle a classroom full of energetic third graders without breaking a sweat. Now she was unraveling before their eyes, her carefully constructed facade crumbling under the weight of terror and helplessness.

Becky tried to calm her down, approaching with the gentle manner of someone used to soothing distressed children, but got her hands slapped away when she got too close. "Anyone have something to calm her?" She glanced back at Tessa with growing concern. "Would you like a glass of wine? It might help you relax."

"No!" Tessa's voice was sharp, almost hysterical. She darted to the bedroom, her movements erratic and unpredictable.

"She's going to do something drastic, Shea." Becky's voice carried the weight of someone who recognized the signs of a complete mental breakdown.

Shea nodded and got to her feet, ignoring the protests from her injured arm. Every movement sent fresh waves of pain through her body, but Tessa's deteriorating mental state was more dangerous than her physical wounds. A panicked person could get them all killed.

"I'll try to talk to her." She made her way down the hall, each step careful and deliberate. Approaching someone in Tessa's state required the same caution as handling an explosive device.

"What are you doing?" Shea found Tessa pulling on a gray hooded sweatshirt with frantic, jerky movements.

"I'm getting out of here. Kara didn't make it. If I do, we have a chance." Tessa's voice was breathless, rushed, as if she was trying to convince herself as much as anyone else.

The logic was flawed, born of desperation rather than rational thought. But Shea could see the determination in her friend's eyes, the desperate hope that movement—any movement—was better than waiting to die.

"Listen to me." Shea put her hands on her friend's shoulders, trying to project calm authority. "You're not thinking clearly. The shock—"

"No!" Tessa shoved her hard, sending Shea stumbling backward into the dresser. The impact jarred her injured arm, sending fresh spikes of agony through her system. "I can't stay here and wait to die. I just can't."

Tears streamed down Tessa's face, but her expression was wild, beyond reason. She looked like a cornered animal, ready to fight anything that tried to stop her escape.

Shea stepped in front of the door, blocking the only exit from the room. "It's too dangerous. It's you against six armed men. Please listen to reason."

"Move or I'll punch you," Tessa growled, her hands clenched into fists. The threat was so unlike her normal personality that it sent chills down Shea's spine.

By now, the others had gathered in the hallway, drawn by the commotion. Fear covered every face as they watched their friend's complete mental collapse. Their pleas mingled with Shea's, creating a chorus of desperate voices trying to reach through the panic that had consumed Tessa's mind.

"Tessa, please think about this," Emma said, her voice shaking. "We need to stick together."

"You're not thinking straight," Rachel added. "The stress is making you—"

Tessa pulled a kitchen knife from under her

sweatshirt, the blade catching the dim light. "Anyone touches me, and I'll cut them."

The sight of the weapon in her friend's trembling hands made everyone step back instinctively. This wasn't the Tessa they knew—this was someone pushed beyond her breaking point, capable of violence they'd never imagined.

"You've lost all your sense." Rachel made a tentative move forward, stopping abruptly when Tessa brandished the knife in her direction. The blade wavered dangerously, held by hands that shook with adrenaline and terror.

"Move back." Tessa's face darkened, her features twisted by emotions she couldn't control. "All of you, just stay away from me."

"Please." Shea held out her hands in a gesture of surrender, trying to project calm she didn't feel. "I can keep you safe. Trust me."

"Nobody can keep us safe. If we stay, we die." Tessa's voice cracked on the words, revealing the depth of her terror. "Don't you understand? They're going to kill us all anyway. At least this way, maybe one of us has a chance."

The logic was twisted but understandable. Trapped animals often chose to run into certain death rather than wait for it to come to them. But Shea couldn't let her friend throw her life away.

She moved to grab Tessa's wrist, hoping to disarm her, and got another cut for her trouble. This one was deeper than her previous wounds, slicing through the sleeve of her shirt and into the flesh beneath. She clutched her arm and stumbled back, feeling warm blood seep between her fingers.

"Please don't do this," she gasped, pain making her voice tight.

"I'm sorry I hurt you." Tessa's expression flickered with momentary regret before the panic reasserted itself. "But I have to go. I have to try."

She ran for the bathroom, pushing past the others with desperate strength. By the time Shea and the others followed, all they could see was the top of her head and a strip of gray sweatshirt she'd left behind on the window frame. Through the open window came the rustling of leaves, then the pounding of footsteps as Tessa crashed through the underbrush.

Shea peered out to see her friend disappear into the trees as the morning sun cast long shadows across the forest floor. Tessa moved erratically, stumbling and weaving like someone drunk or in shock, making no attempt at stealth or concealment.

Less than five minutes later came Tessa's scream. Shrill, desperate, and filled with terror that seemed to echo off the mountains themselves. Shea's heart plummeted as the sound cut through the morning air like a blade.

Her friend pleaded for her life, the words too distant to make out clearly but the tone unmistakable. The desperate bargaining of someone who had realized too late that her escape attempt had been a fatal mistake. Her cries of terror turned to ones of agony, each scream more desperate than the last.

"Oh, God, no." Becky covered her face with her hands, unable to listen to the sounds of their friend's suffering. "We should have stopped her. We should have done something."

As suddenly as the screaming had started, it stopped. The silence that followed was almost worse than the sounds of torture had been, filled with implications too horrible to contemplate.

Shea slumped against the bathroom wall, still clutching the fresh cut Tessa had given her. Blood seeped between her fingers, adding to the collection of wounds she'd accumulated during their ordeal. "Becky, fix me up. I'm going to see if I can help her. Hurry. Don't bother with Band-Aids. Just give me something to wrap around my arm."

"You can't go out there," Annie protested, her voice high with panic. "You heard what happened to her. They'll kill you too."

"She might still be alive." Shea knew it was probably false hope, but she couldn't abandon her friend without trying. "I have to check."

Becky handed her the sleeve torn from a flannel shirt, her hands shaking as she wrapped it around the wound. "Be careful. Don't be next."

"I won't." She gave a promise she prayed she could keep, knowing that hope might be all that kept her friends sane. "Keep the others here in any way you can."

"After hearing Tessa, I don't think any of them will flee." Becky tied the makeshift bandage tightly around Shea's arm, pulling it snug enough to slow the bleeding. "I don't think you'll fit through the window."

"I don't have a choice. The tree is too risky after killing two men. If they haven't figured out how I got out, they will soon." Shea looked at her friends, trying to memorize their faces in case this was the last time she saw them alive. "Keep that back door locked."

She'd have a tough time getting out the small bathroom window, but it would be impossible for a full-grown man to fit through. That fact alone might save her friends' lives if her rescue attempt failed.

She glanced at the faces of her friends, imprinting them on her mind. They were why she had to try and help Tessa, even if the odds were hopeless. These women had been her sisters for over a decade, and she wouldn't abandon any of them without a fight.

"Here." Annie handed her the inhaler with trembling fingers. "You left it on the couch."

"Thanks." Shea took a shuddering breath and slipped the device into her pocket, hoping she wouldn't need it when stealth was essential. "I love you girls. Keep watch for me. When you see me, create a distraction."

The words felt like a farewell, weighted with the possibility that she might not return. But someone had to try, and she was the only one with the training and experience to have any chance of success.

She climbed onto the toilet and began the painful process of squeezing through the window. Her injured arms protested every movement, but she wiggled and sucked in her gut until she managed to get through, leaving traces of blood on the windowsill. At this rate, there wouldn't be much of her left when they were finally free.

"Psst." Becky's voice came from behind her as she prepared to run for the tree line. Her friend tossed a water bottle and a granola bar out the window. "Just in case."

The supplies were a practical gift, acknowledgment that this rescue attempt might take longer than expected. Shea nodded her thanks and made a dash for the trees in the direction Tessa had gone, following the obvious trail of broken branches and disturbed undergrowth her panicked friend had left behind.

The forest felt different in daylight, less mysterious but more ominous. Every shadow could hide an armed man, every sound could signal an ambush. She moved as quietly as possible, using skills learned from years of hunting with her father before he'd abandoned them.

The further in she went, the easier it was to decipher where the men might've taken Tessa. The clearing with its ritualistic symbols and bloodstained altar—of course that's where they'd go. The place was designed for exactly this kind of horror.

She paused frequently to listen for sounds of pursuit, but heard nothing except the normal sounds of the forest. Not even birds were singing, as if nature itself recoiled from the evil that had passed this way. The silence was oppressive, heavy with the weight of violence and suffering.

As she neared the clearing, she stopped again, pressing herself against a large oak tree. Her heart beat so hard she thought anyone close would be able to hear it hammering against her ribs. The sound seemed impossibly loud in the unnatural quiet.

No voices came to her ears. No screams or cries. Just a heavy presence that threatened to take her breath away, an almost physical weight of malevolence that made her skin crawl.

Shea stepped from the brush and onto the trail, every nerve alert for danger. A few feet further, she entered the clearing and immediately saw what she'd feared and hoped against.

Tessa lay on the rock altar, positioned exactly like a sacrificial victim from some ancient ritual. A knife protruded from her chest, the blade driven deep between her ribs. The first sacrifice to whatever demon the group of men served, her blood already beginning to stain the rust-colored rock beneath her.

Fearing the worst but hoping against hope, Shea approached her friend with careful steps. Her heart stopped as Tessa moaned softly, the sound barely audible but unmistakably alive.

She was alive. Hurt, probably dying, but alive.

Shea rushed forward, abandoning caution in favor of speed. Tessa's eyes fluttered open, unfocused and glazed with pain. "Help me," she whispered, the words barely audible.

"I will." Shea assessed the wound quickly, her first aid training taking over. She didn't want to remove the knife, fearing her friend would bleed out, but she couldn't get her back to the cabin with it sticking out of her chest like a gruesome flagpole.

She removed the cleaner bandage from where Becky had closed her own wound with Band-Aids. It wasn't much, but it was the best she could do under the circumstances.

"This is going to hurt," she warned, gripping the knife handle with both hands. The metal was slick with blood, making her grip uncertain.

She yanked it free with one swift motion, and Tessa's scream filled the clearing, echoing off the surrounding trees with heart-wrenching intensity.

"Shh. We don't want them coming back." Shea pressed the bandage against the wound, trying to stem the flow of blood that immediately began seeping through the fabric. "Hold this tight."

She went in search of moss, remembering wilderness first aid techniques from her youth. The plant would help absorb blood and might have some natural antiseptic properties. She pulled some from under a nearby tree, where it grew thick and green in the shade.

She placed the moss against the wound, using the now bloody bandage to hold it in place. It was primitive medicine, but it might buy them enough time to get back to the cabin.

"I'm going to help you off the altar. We have to be as quiet as possible, okay?" She supported Tessa's weight as her friend struggled to sit up.

Tessa nodded weakly. "I'm sorry. I'm so sorry I ran. I was so scared."

"No apology necessary." Shea helped her friend get to her feet, then propped an arm under her shoulder. "We all do things when we're afraid. The important thing is getting you back safely."

"I don't think I can do this." Tessa sobbed, her legs barely supporting her weight. "I'm too weak. Leave me here."

"Yes, you can." Shea's voice was firm, brooking no argument. "You fight through or die here. Those are your only choices."

The sun now hung high in the sky, making their journey back more dangerous. Getting to the cabin would be tricky with daylight exposure and Tessa's condition slowing them down significantly.

Tessa's breathing had become labored, each step requiring tremendous effort. Her weight grew heavier as she leaned more heavily on Shea for support. Shea really wasn't in the condition she needed to be in to help a severely injured person, but she had no choice.

Why wasn't Tessa dead? The question nagged at her as they struggled through the forest. Had she been left as a warning, or did the men intend for her to slowly bleed to death? So many questions and no answers, but the important thing was that her friend was alive.

They had to stop several times to rest, each pause making Shea worry they'd be discovered. She couldn't fight anyone as hurt as she was, with one barely functional arm and another person depending on her for survival. She'd have to use her gun if they were attacked, and the sound would give their position away to anyone within earshot.

"Stop, please." Tessa's voice was weak, barely above a whisper.

Shea stopped, supporting her friend's weight as Tessa bent over.

Tessa vomited into the bushes, her body rejecting what little food she'd managed to eat. She swiped her hand across her mouth with shaking fingers. "Okay, I'm ready."

"You sure?" Shea searched her friend's pale face for signs of consciousness and determination.

"Yes, just get me back. I'm sorry I cut you, and sorry I ran. I'm such a fool."

"No, just scared." Shea adjusted her grip, taking more of Tessa's weight. "People do things when they're afraid that they'd never do otherwise. What matters is that you're alive."

"You're going to be a great sheriff," Tessa said between labored breaths. "You have exactly the right instincts for it."

"Thanks." The words meant more than Tessa could know, coming from someone who'd seen her at her worst and still believed in her abilities. They resumed their slow trek down the trail, every step a small victory.

At the edge of the tree line, Shea stopped and studied the open ground between them and the cabin. Too much exposure, too much risk of being seen by their watchers. When Becky spotted them through a gap in the window coverings, Shea waved frantically, then ducked out of sight behind a large pine tree.

A few minutes later, screams and loud arguing came from the cabin, the sounds of what appeared to be a major fight between the trapped women. Laughter rang out from the front of the building as the men believed the stress of the situation had caused the women to turn on each other.

The distraction was perfect, exactly what Shea had hoped for from her resourceful friends.

"We have to run now," she told Tessa. "Can you do it?"

"Let's do it." Tessa straightened as much as her injuries allowed, summoning reserves of strength she didn't know she had.

They ran in a shambling, desperate sprint toward

the bathroom window. Someone inside had the foresight to look for a rope of some kind and had tossed out a thick, white curtain tie-back, the kind used for heavy drapes.

"I can't climb that." Tessa's eyes widened as she looked at the makeshift rope hanging from the window. "I'm too weak."

Shea would have a difficult time herself with her injured arms, but there was no alternative. "You have to. There's no other way."

Tessa took a deep breath and began to "walk" her way slowly up the wall while Shea kept watch, her gun ready in case their desperate sprint had been noticed. The climb seemed to take an eternity when it really only took a few minutes, each second stretching like hours as Shea expected to hear shouts or gunfire.

Then it was Shea's turn. The arm sporting the two cuts had started to bleed again from the exertion, making her grip slippery on the improvised rope. The pain was excruciating, but she forced herself to climb, pulling herself up hand over hand until friendly arms reached down to haul her through the window.

Once she fell into the bathroom, she pulled the rope in after her and collapsed on the tiled floor next to Tessa. Both women lay there gasping, their energy completely spent.

She stared up into the worried faces of her friends bending over them, feeling a wave of gratitude so intense it brought tears to her eyes. "Just give us a few minutes."

"I'll get what medical supplies we have left." Becky rushed from the room, already shifting into caretaker mode.

If help didn't come soon, they'd be in dire straits. Shea's energy had bled out onto the tiled floor along with her blood, and she wasn't sure how much more punishment her body could take. Tessa seemed only marginally better, the moss doing its job of absorbing blood but doing nothing for the underlying damage.

"I could use a glass of wine," Shea said, trying to inject some levity into the grim situation.

Tessa turned her head to look at her friend. "Me, too. A very large glass."

"Coming right up." Emma rushed away, grateful to have something concrete to do. By the time Becky returned with their dwindling medical supplies, they each held a glass of wine, the alcohol providing some small comfort in their desperate situation.

"Once I've done my medical work," Becky said, already assessing their wounds with professional efficiency, "it's into bed with both of you. If you don't get some sleep, Shea, you'll be useless. Our barricades are holding. You don't need to sit up twenty-four-seven."

She could use the rest more than she cared to admit. With Tessa having run off and nearly died, the men would expect another woman to panic and try to escape. They'd probably bide their time, smoking and drinking their beer, confident that fear would do their work for them.

For a time, at least, until boredom set in and they decided to escalate their attacks.

A time would come when the men's assaults would grow fiercer, and Shea needed to be ready for that moment.

"What happened to you out there, Tessa?" Becky frowned at the moss and bandage arrangement covering the chest wound. "This is... creative first aid."

"That would be Shea's doing," Tessa said weakly. "She saved my life."

"I had to stop the bleeding." Shea sat up carefully and scooted her back against the bathtub for support. "They had her on the altar in that clearing we found."

"They were going to watch as I died," Tessa continued, her voice gaining strength as she spoke. "But something spooked them. Something was crashing through the brush. I thought I'd be eaten by a bear or some demon from hell they were sacrificing me to."

Her tears started anew as the full horror of her experience sank in. "We can't leave. We have to wait until help comes. I see that now."

"Kara made it," Emma said firmly, crossing her arms. "We didn't hear any screaming from her direction."

That didn't necessarily mean anything, but Shea let the comment stand. Her friends had been through enough without worrying that Kara might be lying dead in the woods somewhere. She would cling to hope until there was nothing left to hold onto.

After Becky finished her medical work, Shea climbed into bed and fell into an exhausted sleep. When she woke, the sun had started to set, painting the cabin in shades of orange and red that reminded her uncomfortably of blood.

She tried to remember if this was their second night or their third. Second, she thought. Kara might've reached the gas station by now, assuming she hadn't gotten lost or been caught. If not, surely by the third night, someone would come looking for them.

Unless Kara had gotten lost in unfamiliar territory. How well could she navigate through dense forest she'd never seen before, especially in the dark?

The questions multiplied without answers, each one adding to the weight of uncertainty that pressed down on them all.

She groaned and sat up, dangling her legs over the side of the bed and waiting for the dizziness to pass. When she could stand without wobbling, she headed to the living room as the others prepared for bed.

"I made sandwiches," Becky said, gesturing toward the kitchen. "Yours is in the fridge."

"Thanks." Shea ate the ham and cheese mechanically, tasting nothing, while waiting for a pot of coffee to brew. Food was fuel now, nothing more.

She didn't mind taking the night shift. The others needed their rest as much as she'd needed hers. Who knew how long until the men stopped playing psychological games and fought to get inside the cabin?

They'd have to fight for their lives at that point, and Shea was the only one with any real combat experience. How much good could she do with one barely functional arm and a body that was running on fumes?

Chapter Seven

Deborah glared at Becky over breakfast that morning, her face twisted with anger and exhaustion. "This is all your fault." Her voice trembled with barely contained rage.

The statement stopped Shea's movement toward the bedroom to catch some sleep. She turned slowly, feeling the weight of tension that had been building among the group finally exploding into the open. "What did you say?"

Deborah shrugged, her usually composed financial advisor demeanor completely shattered. "I think you heard me."

The accusation hung in the air like poison gas. After everything they'd been through together, after watching Melanie die and nearly losing Tessa, they started to turn on each other. Shea had seen it before in crisis situations—when people were pushed beyond their breaking point, they needed someone to blame, and the easiest target was often the person closest to them.

"Why would you say that?" Tears welled in Becky's eyes, her face crumpling with hurt and guilt. She'd been holding the group together with sheer force of will, and now one of her oldest friends was attacking her.

"You rented this place. If you'd chosen somewhere else, we wouldn't be in this mess." Deborah's voice rose, years of suppressed frustrations pouring out in a torrent of blame. "You always have to plan everything, control everything. Well, look how that worked out."

"The price was good and the cabin gorgeous in the photos." Becky hung her head. "I thought I was doing something nice for everyone."

Shea could see her friend starting to crumble under the weight of misplaced guilt. Becky had already been dealing with her marital problems, and now she was being blamed for their current nightmare. It was exactly the kind of psychological breakdown their attackers were hoping for.

"It's no one's fault but those twisted men out there." Shea tried to cross her arms and failed as the movement pulled on the wounds covering her left arm. The pain was a sharp reminder of just how much they'd all sacrificed already. "We can't turn on each other." She eyed each of the women at the table, making sure her message was clear. "That's what they want—for us to destroy ourselves from the inside."

The truth was harsh but necessary. Their enemies

were experts at psychological warfare, and internal discord would be more effective than any weapon in breaking down their defenses.

"I'm going to check on Tessa, then try and catch a few hours of sleep. Then, we've got work to do." She kept her voice steady, projecting the authority that came with her badge even though she felt anything but authoritative.

"What kind of work?" Emma glanced up from the piece of toast on a napkin in front of her. She'd barely eaten anything since Melanie's death, and her face was gaunt with stress and grief.

"Booby traps." The words felt strange in her mouth, but she'd come to accept that survival sometimes required thinking like the enemy. It was only a matter of time before the men tried to get inside the cabin. She wanted to leave a few nasty surprises for them. She and the other women would need every advantage they could get against trained killers.

"Booby traps?" Annie's voice rose an octave. "You mean like in the movies?"

"Exactly like in the movies, except these will be real and they'll be designed to kill or maim anyone who tries to get in here uninvited." Shea's voice was matter-of-fact, but she could see the shock on her friends' faces. The sweet, law-abiding woman they'd known in college was talking about setting lethal traps with the casual efficiency of a soldier.

Tessa softly snored when Shea checked on her,

exhaustion having finally overcome pain and fear. The fresh strip of torn sheet showed that Becky had tended to her wound before going to the kitchen to face Deborah's accusations. Even in crisis, Becky couldn't stop taking care of everyone else.

Sleep took a while to overtake Shea as her mind spun with possibilities for the kind of traps she could construct with their limited resources. She wasn't sure how much help the others would be—most of them had never held a weapon more dangerous than a kitchen knife—but putting them to work helping her would hopefully keep them from spiraling further into despair. Hope and determination were all they had to get them out alive.

She stared at the ceiling, watching shadows move as clouds passed over the moon outside. She hadn't prayed in a long time, not since her father had abandoned them and left her questioning whether God cared about people like her. But she sent up a quick prayer anyway, just in case someone was listening. If divine intervention was available, now would be a good time for it to kick in.

A few minutes later, her eyes drifted closed, and she fell into a restless sleep filled with dreams of running through dark forests while invisible predators hunted her.

When she woke several hours later, Tessa smiled at her from the other bed, though the expression was strained with pain. "We're a pair, aren't we?"

Shea yawned, stretching carefully to avoid aggravating her injuries, and sat up. "We look like we've been in a war." The observation was more accurate than she'd intended—they had been in a war, just not the conventional kind. "You okay?"

"If I don't move much." Tessa's voice was stronger than it had been earlier, suggesting that rest and Becky's medical attention were helping her recover.

"Then don't move."

"I need to use the restroom." The admission came with obvious embarrassment—basic bodily functions had become complicated when every movement was agony.

Shea got to her feet, suppressing a groan as her own injuries protested. "I'll help you, then it's back to bed for you." She studied her friend's face, noting the pallor beneath her dark skin and the lines of pain around her eyes. "I want you to promise me something."

"Anything. I owe you my life." Tessa's gratitude was evident in every word.

"When those men get in—not if, when—I want you to hide under the bed. As far back as possible so they don't see you." Shea's voice was gentle but firm. She wasn't asking for a favor; she was giving an order.

Tessa's face went pale despite her darker complexion. "You think they will." It wasn't a question.

"I know they will." The certainty in her voice came from years of law enforcement experience and an understanding of predator psychology. These men were patient, but they wouldn't wait forever. Eventually, they'd want to end their game. "They're just playing with us right now, but that won't last."

She helped Tessa to the bathroom and waited while her friend relieved herself and brushed her teeth—small acts of normalcy that felt both precious and absurd given their circumstances. Then she helped her back to bed, noting how much effort even these simple movements required.

"Promise me," Shea insisted as she tucked the quilt around Tessa's shoulders.

"I promise. They won't get me again." Tessa reached under her pillow and pulled out something that made Shea's eyes widen. A blood-stained knife lay there—the very weapon that had nearly killed her in the ritual clearing. "I have the very one they tried to kill me with."

"That's my girl." Shea smiled with genuine pride. Her friend was tougher than anyone had given her credit for. She rejoined the others in the front room, ready to begin their preparations. "Here's the plan—"

Becky was staring out the window, her face pale with confusion. "What?" Shea's smile faded as she recognized the expression of someone who'd just discovered something impossible.

"They're gone."

"What?" Shea joined her at the window, pushing aside the edge of the blanket they'd used to block the view. Sure enough, the trucks that had been their constant companions were nowhere to be seen. No armed guard patrolled out front. The area looked completely deserted, almost peaceful in the morning light.

Did she dare hope they'd given up, or were they waiting for the women to leave the safety of the cabin? Every instinct told her it was too good to be true, but the evidence was right in front of her eyes.

"I'm going out." Becky moved toward the heavy bookcase they'd positioned in front of the door, her movements quick with desperate hope.

"No. Let me." Shea held out a hand to stop her. If this was a trap—which it almost certainly was—she was the only one with the training to survive it potentially.

"You're needed more." Becky's logic was sound but flawed. She was thinking tactically when she should have been thinking emotionally.

"We need you, too. You're the mother of us all." It was true—Becky had been holding them together with her practical competence and caring nature. Losing her would destroy the group's cohesion.

"I'll go." Rachel spoke from the sofa where she'd been sitting with her arms wrapped around her knees. "I don't have anyone waiting for me at home."

The statement was heartbreaking in its simple honesty. While the others had husbands, children, and careers that gave their lives meaning, Rachel had always felt like she was on the periphery of life, watching others live while she existed.

Shea shook her head firmly. "I don't think they've gone. It's a trap." Every fiber of her law enforcement training screamed warnings. Predators didn't just give up when they had cornered prey.

"You don't know that." Rachel got to her feet and helped Becky move the bookcase, her movements determined despite her apparent fear. "Maybe they got bored. Maybe they found something else to hunt."

When they had moved the obstacle aside, Rachel put a hand on the doorknob and glanced over her shoulder at her friends. "Love you girls."

"Ditto," they said in unison, the word carrying the weight of a final goodbye.

Shea moved to the window, squeezing behind the mattress they'd used as additional protection. She held her gun in her right hand, the weight familiar and comforting. "I'll provide cover if I can. If you make it out of the drive, we'll follow."

It was a lie, and they all knew it. If Rachel made it past whatever trap was waiting, the rest of them would still be too smart to follow. But sometimes lies were kinder than the truth.

Rachel nodded and opened the door slowly, as if expecting it to explode in her face. She hesitated for a long moment, gathering courage, then stepped onto the porch with the careful movements of someone walking through a minefield.

A shot rang out almost immediately, the sound sharp and final in the morning air. The bullet spun Rachel around like a dancer, and she dropped back into the cabin with blood spreading across her shoulder.

"Get that door closed! They've got a sniper somewhere out there." Shea rushed to Rachel's side, her medical training taking over as she assessed the wound. The shot had caught her friend in the shoulder—painful and debilitating, but not immediately life-threatening if they could stop the bleeding.

"Bind her up, Becky." She helped push the bookcase back against the door until it stood once again as their primary barrier against the outside world.

The trap had been simple but effective. Present a safe opportunity for escape, then punish anyone foolish enough to take it. The psychological impact was devastating—they'd tried to leave and been shot down like animals.

"I need every kitchen knife, nail, and anything that can be carved into spikes. If you can find rope, I also need that. Put everything on the table." Shea's voice carried new urgency. The sniper meant their enemies were still very much present and very much in control. "If you find something we might be able to use that I haven't mentioned, add it to the pile."

She marched to the back door, her mind already working through defensive possibilities. First priority would be securing the deck. If she could use the tree to get down, so could those men.

She eyed the Adirondack chairs scattered around the deck furniture. "Deborah, come help me."

"What do you need?" Deborah's earlier anger had been replaced by fear and a grudging recognition that Shea was their best hope for survival.

"Help me drag those chairs inside. I can use the wood for stakes." The furniture was solid pine, perfect for creating the kind of defensive obstacles she had in mind.

"You have to go out there again if you're going to set traps." The observation carried obvious concern for Shea's safety.

"I know. Most of the traps will be inside the house, but I need to keep them from gaining access to the deck." She dragged one chair inside with her good arm while Deborah managed the others. The wood would be perfect for creating defensive spikes once they broke it down into manageable pieces.

Once they had all four chairs inside, Shea asked for the hammer and the reciprocating saw they'd found earlier. The tools felt heavy in her hands—not just because of their physical weight, but because of what she was planning to do with them.

"Be right back." Deborah rushed off, returning a minute later with the requested items and an expression of grim determination.

"What else can we do?" Emma came down the hall, her usually perfect appearance disheveled, but her eyes showed new resolve.

"Break the bathroom mirror into as many two-inch shards as possible, then put them in a bag I can carry over my shoulder." Her plans would take time and coordination. She prayed the men would stay away long enough for them to complete their preparations.

The sound of breaking glass from the bathroom told her that Emma followed her instructions. Each crash was like a small explosion, marking another step in their transformation from victims to combatants.

"Have you ever done this sort of thing before?" Deborah asked as she began dismantling one of the chairs with the hammer.

"No, just read about it online." The admission might have been embarrassing under normal circumstances, but desperation had a way of making experts out of amateurs. "Military survival forums, mostly. You'd be amazed at what people share on the internet."

The drone of the saw cut off any further conversation as Shea struggled to work with only one functional arm. The vibration sent shocks of pain through her injuries, but she gritted her teeth and continued.

"Let me." Deborah took her place at the saw, her movements more efficient than Shea's had been. "I'm perfectly capable of making spikes. Where are you going to put them?"

"Under all the windows." The placement would create a nasty surprise for anyone trying to climb through their makeshift barricades.

"That sniper..." Deborah's voice trailed off, but the concern was clear.

"It's a chance I have to take." Shea knew the risk, but without defensive measures, they were just sitting ducks waiting to be shot. "If we don't make this place dangerous for them, they'll walk in here and kill us at their leisure."

Leaving Deborah to form the wooden spikes, Shea returned to the dining room to inventory their other resources. Fishing line from someone's tackle box, metal cans with their contents poured into bowls, six steak knives they'd gathered from the kitchen—it wasn't much, but creative desperation could make weapons out of almost anything.

"Anyone think they can form a giant spider web out of that fishing line?" She held up the nearly invisible filament, envisioning the possibilities.

"I can." Annie raised her hand tentatively. "I used to make my own fishing nets when I was a kid."

"Good. Make two if you have enough line. Scatter as many fishhooks as you can throughout them." The fishing hooks would turn the nearly invisible barriers into flesh-shredding obstacles. "I want to hang one at the end of the hall to protect the bedrooms and the other across the front door."

She explained her vision while Annie worked, seeing understanding dawn in her friend's eyes. The traps wouldn't stop determined attackers, but they might slow them down enough to give the defenders a fighting chance.

"While I'm outside laying the perimeter traps, I want each of you to find a place to hide if we're breached. A place where, if they find you, you can attack by surprise." She looked at each woman in turn, seeing fear but also growing determination. "Tessa and Rachel will hide under the beds behind our suitcases."

"We can do this." Becky squared her shoulders, the old competent organizer reasserting herself despite everything they'd been through. "I'll string the cans together with the remaining fishing line. It'll give us a warning system, at least."

"Good thinking." Shea gave her a look of approval, grateful to see her friend's natural leadership abilities returning. "If they can't sneak up on us, then we'll be ready." As ready as a group of college friends could be against trained killers.

"Here's the glass." Emma handed her a small vinyl backpack; the kind children used for school supplies. The irony wasn't lost on any of them—they were preparing for war using the tools of everyday life.

"I'm going to..." Becky's voice faltered for a moment. "I'm moving Melanie's body to the hall closet. We don't want her to start... you know."

Shea understood. In the stress of survival, they'd been avoiding the practical reality of death. A body left unattended in warm conditions would begin to decompose, creating health hazards and psychological trauma they didn't need to deal with.

She exhaled heavily. "I'm going out to place stakes under the windows, then fix the tree so they can't get to the deck. I need someone to watch my back."

"I will," Becky said without hesitation. "I'll move to every window you're working under. Don't get shot."

"I'm hoping not to. That's why I'm waiting until nightfall." The sun was already beginning to set—she'd slept most of the day away, but the rest had been necessary to function.

"But your arm." Emma stared at the bandages that were beginning to show fresh blood seepage. "You can barely use it."

"I'll be okay." Shea made herself a quick sandwich, mechanically chewing food that tasted like cardboard, then slipped a few extra bullets into her pocket. She also pocketed the military knife, its weight both comforting and ominous.

She prepared herself mentally for what might be her final mission. What she needed was a miracle in the form of a rescue party, but she'd settle for the miracle of getting back into the cabin in one piece.

As soon as the sun set and darkness provided some cover, she tossed the wooden spikes out the back window, then carried the bag of glass shards, nails, and hammer onto the deck. Becky followed with her gun in hand, her face set with determination.

"Close this door behind me and don't open it unless you hear the code word." Shea thought quickly.

"Butterfly. If I don't say butterfly, don't let me in."

Her friend nodded. "Be careful out there."

"I will." Shea made the familiar climb down the tree, pausing at the bottom to listen for any signs that she'd been detected. No shots rang out, but that didn't mean she wasn't being watched.

Staying close to the shadow of the cabin, she started placing the wooden spikes in the ground, burying them just deep enough that they wouldn't be easily seen but would still be effective against anyone trying to approach the windows. She wished she could set explosives, but that required skills and materials she didn't have.

She perspired despite the cool autumn night, using the neckline of her already filthy T-shirt to wipe sweat and blood from her face. The cuts on her arm throbbed with each movement, and fresh blood soaked through Becky's careful bandaging. She bit her lip against the pain and continued working.

Her heart stopped at every rustle of leaves, every snap of a twig. Was she being watched, or did the sniper only cover the front of the cabin? She figured they probably thought the women were too smart to go out the back again—not after what had happened to Tessa. They'd expect the rest to try the front door, just like Rachel had.

Once the spikes were placed around the cabin's perimeter, she scattered dead leaves over them to camouflage their presence. Deborah had done an excellent job of sharpening the tips—they'd slow down anyone trying to reach the windows and might even disable an attacker if they stepped wrong.

That job complete, she turned her attention to the tree. Using the hammer, she drove nails into the trunk at regular intervals, sharp points facing outward like a medieval torture device. When she reached the branch that hung over the deck, she began the delicate process of jabbing glass shards into the bark as she crawled backward along the limb.

The work was painstaking and dangerous. One slip would send her plummeting to the ground below, and the glass cut her hands even as she embedded it in the tree. By the time she'd finished, her stomach was scraped raw from the rough bark, and there wasn't much left of her black T-shirt.

She'd effectively stopped her own tree-climbing route as much as she'd prevented anyone else from using it. The branch was now a gauntlet of sharp obstacles that would shred anyone trying to traverse it.

She chuckled grimly despite the direness of their situation. At this rate, she'd have to wear the ridiculous pink shirt before long—it was the only clean garment she had left.

Becky had the door open before Shea's feet touched the deck, as if she'd been watching through the glass the entire time. "You're like a female James Bond," she said with admiration.

"Let's hope it works." Shea stepped inside

gratefully, locking the door behind her and checking the simple alarm system they'd rigged.

"How long do you think we have before they make their move?" Becky's question carried the weight of someone trying to plan for an unknowable future.

"I don't know. The waiting could be part of their psychological game." Shea considered the possibilities. "Or maybe they have families they need to get home to and they'll be back tomorrow."

The thought was chilling in its mundane horror. What would their families think if they knew about the games these men played with unsuspecting renters? Maybe they did know and were just as sick and twisted as the hunters themselves.

"I'm going to get cleaned up. You and the others should try to get some sleep. I'll retake the night watch." She felt responsible for keeping her friends safe, even though she knew her injuries were slowing her down.

"I can sit up with you," Becky offered. "You shouldn't have to do everything alone."

"No, get some rest. I'll be fine." She needed the quiet time to think, to plan, to prepare mentally for what was almost certainly coming.

"We've only got two more days of food, Shea." Worry creased Becky's brow as she contemplated their dwindling supplies.

"We'll have to ration what we have." The thought of starvation was just another layer of pressure, but she hoped they wouldn't be here that long. "Kara had to have made it down the mountain by now."

She refused to believe anything else. Help would come—it had to. All they had to do was hold on long enough for rescue to arrive.

She ducked carefully under the fishing line trap at the end of the hall and made her way to the bathroom. She tossed her ruined shirt on the floor and washed as well as she could without taking a full shower—the sound of running water might mask approaching footsteps.

When she'd finished cleaning up, she changed into her last black T-shirt, eyeing the pink monstrosity shoved into her bag. "It's going to be you and me again soon, my pink nightmare," she muttered.

She tiptoed past the bedroom where Rachel and Tessa lay recovering from their wounds, then glanced up the stairs toward where she knew the others were trying to sleep. Rest easy, my friends, she thought. You'll need every bit of strength you can gather.

With a heavy sigh, she settled into a kitchen chair positioned to face the front door, her gun across her lap, and began another long vigil. Outside, the forest was silent except for the normal sounds of nocturnal creatures going about their business.

But somewhere out there, she knew, patient predators were waiting for their moment to strike.

Chapter Eight

Something slammed against the front door with the force of a battering ram. Shea tensed, every muscle in her body coiling like a spring as the sound reverberated through the cabin. Glass shattered somewhere on the other side of the side window, the noise muffled by the mattress they'd positioned as a barrier but still clearly audible.

The sound she'd been dreading had finally come. After hours of psychological warfare, waiting, and preparation, their enemies made their move.

Within minutes, the other women—minus Tessa and Rachel, who were still recovering from their wounds—had congregated in the living room. They moved with purpose despite their fear, each grabbing a weapon from their improvised arsenal. Deborah hefted one of the leftover wooden spikes, testing its weight and balance. Annie gripped a heavy flashlight like a club, its metal body substantial enough to do real damage. Becky held her gun with both hands, though

Shea could see the tremor in her grip. Lauren clutched the fireplace poker with white-knuckled grip, and Emma had grabbed the fire extinguisher from under the kitchen sink, its red cylinder surprisingly heavy.

All the kitchen knives, other than the one Shea carried in her pocket, had been used in their trap construction. They'd committed everything to this defense.

Shea got to her feet, feeling the weight of leadership settle on her shoulders like a lead blanket. The others formed a defensive half-circle behind her, looking to her for guidance in a situation none of them had ever imagined facing.

"They're going to get in, ladies." Her voice was steady despite the fear churning in her stomach. "Fight with everything you have. Remember, these men killed Melanie. They tortured Tessa. They shot Rachel. Show them no mercy, because they'll show you none."

The reminder of what they'd already lost had hardened the women's expressions, transforming fear into something more useful—anger.

"Becky, please go tell Tessa and Rachel to get under the beds." Shea wanted their wounded friends as far from the coming violence as possible.

Her friend rushed to do Shea's bidding, her footsteps quick on the hardwood floor. She returned within moments, her face flushed with exertion and worry. "I made sure they were pressed up against the walls and that the suitcases completely hid them." Her voice shook slightly. "They're probably safer than the rest of us."

Shea agreed. Another window shattered, the sound of breaking glass mixing with the splintering of wood as their barricades were systematically destroyed. The women turned as one toward the new threat.

Footsteps crunched through dry leaves outside the compromised window, deliberate and unhurried. The men circled the cabin like wolves, taking their time to ensure no escape route remained open. The bookcase in front of the door began to move inch by inch as more than one man pushed against it from the outside.

A howl of pain suddenly erupted from somewhere near the front of the cabin, followed by creative cursing that would have made a sailor blush. "Careful, y'all, they've set traps out here! I've gouged my foot clean through on a spike."

Shea smiled grimly at her friends. "One down, at least temporarily."

"I hope they all fall on those spikes," Becky said through gritted teeth, her gun aimed steadily at the front door.

"I hope they die." Emma's quietly spoken wish hung heavy in the air, shocking everyone with its venom. Sweet Emma, who wouldn't hurt a fly under normal circumstances, had been pushed beyond her breaking point.

"If we can survive until tomorrow afternoon," Deborah said, her voice carrying desperate hope, "people will realize something is wrong. I'm supposed to be back to work tomorrow night. I've never missed a shift without calling in, not once in eight years. "

"Bill will call by nightfall if I haven't picked up the boys from soccer practice," Becky added. "He might be angry with me, but he'd never let anything happen to them. When I don't show up..."

"But we don't have cell service up here," Lauren pointed out, her eyes widening with sudden inspiration. "Why don't we leave voicemails on our phones explaining the situation? When someone calls and we don't answer, they'll hear the messages."

Why hadn't Shea thought of that? Sometimes the simplest solutions were the most effective. "Do it now, quickly."

She grabbed her phone off the kitchen table, grateful she'd left it there rather than in the bedroom. The battery was nearly dead, but she had just enough power to change her voicemail greeting. "This is Sheriff Callahan. We're trapped at a rental cabin on Misty Mountain. A group of armed men have surrounded us in some kind of sick hunting game. We have one dead and two wounded. There are seven survivors." She rattled off the address and everyone's names, speaking clearly despite the chaos erupting around them.

The current sheriff of Misty Hollow was bound to find out why his new hire didn't show up for work in a day or two. That connection alone might save their lives.

She faced her friends as they finished their own desperate messages. "This will work. I know it will. All we have to do is hold on long enough for people to start missing us."

"Almost twenty-four hours," Deborah whispered hoarsely. "Seems like an eternity."

"We got this." Emma aimed the extinguisher at one of the windows, her grip steady despite everything they'd been through. "We're not the same women who came here for a relaxing weekend. We're fighters now."

Shea had never been prouder of her friends. Despite the fatigue, pain, and overwhelming odds, they stood ready to defend themselves and each other. Pushing aside her exhaustion and the throbbing agony in her injured arm, she positioned herself to face whoever came through that door.

The front door opened a few more inches, stopped by the bookcase but allowing a voice to carry clearly into the cabin. "You're quite the smart one, Sheriff. Setting all these traps."

"Darryl." She recognized the voice from their earlier conversation through the door.

"Y'all ladies ready to play our final game?" His tone was conversational, almost friendly, which made it infinitely more chilling.

"Bring it on." Shea's response was steady, projecting more confidence than she felt.

It wasn't until another mattress fell from a window with a crash and another man cried out in pain, that

Shea realized Darryl planned to distract her with conversation while his men gained entry through other routes. More curses and shouts of agony echoed from multiple directions as his followers encountered her carefully placed traps. None of the obstacles were designed to kill—she wasn't a soldier, just a sheriff trying to protect innocent people. But they would maim and slow the attackers down, hopefully giving the women a fighting chance.

A big brute of a man climbed through the side window, his massive frame filling the opening. Since he didn't limp or show obvious signs of injury, Shea suspected he'd climbed over his wounded comrade to get inside. Another man, smaller but equally dangerous-looking, did the same at the opposite window. The front door stopped its inward movement—apparently, Darryl had decided subtlety was no longer necessary.

A shrill scream, then a heavy thud came from the direction of the back deck. Shea bit back a grin of savage satisfaction. Someone had tried to gain access via her tree route and discovered her glass-and-nail modifications the hard way. That was at least one attacker who might be too injured to pose an immediate threat.

Becky fired her weapon, but her shaking hands sent the shot wide, embedding in the window frame. Her target dove behind the couch for cover, cursing creatively.

"There's only six women in here, boss," he yelled

toward the front door.

"Where are the others, Sheriff?" Darryl's voice carried clearly from behind the bookcase.

"Gone." She forced a laugh that sounded more confident than she felt. "You weren't able to catch them all. Some of us are smarter than you gave us credit for."

"I guess we'll have to settle for the six of you then." His voice carried disappointed resignation, as if he was settling for a lesser meal than he'd hoped for.

Another man entered through the window, his foot wrapped in what looked like a torn flannel shirt—evidence that her spike traps had found their mark. Soon four armed men faced six desperate women in the confined space of the living room. Shea knew she couldn't shoot them all, not before they overwhelmed her friends.

She raised her gun to fire at the nearest threat, only to have Darryl suddenly burst from behind the bookcase and tackle her to the floor with the practiced efficiency of someone who'd done this before. Her weapon skittered across the hardwood and disappeared under the sofa, beyond her immediate reach.

Emma screamed and let loose with the fire extinguisher directly into a bearded man's face, the chemical foam blinding him instantly. Lauren rushed forward with her fireplace poker raised high like a medieval weapon. Chaos erupted throughout the room as the desperate women fought for their lives.

The men seemed to have underestimated their

opponents, entering without firearms and expecting easy prey. That overconfidence was proving to be a costly mistake.

Annie's terrified scream drew Shea's attention away from her own struggle. One of the attackers had grabbed the petite woman around the waist and was dragging her toward the back of the cabin. Deborah took off after them, wooden spike raised like a spear, her face transformed by protective fury.

"Get off me!" Shea kicked out desperately as Darryl's hands reached for her throat. When he wrapped his fingers around her neck, she managed to get her legs around his waist and use his own momentum to flip him onto his back.

He retaliated by punching her directly in her wounded left arm, sending explosions of agony through her entire body. Tears of pain welled in her eyes, and she scrambled for the knife in her pocket as she found herself back on the bottom, his weight pinning her down.

Emma appeared above them like an avenging angel, bringing the heavy fire extinguisher down on Darryl's head with both hands. The impact knocked him off Shea, leaving him dazed and bleeding.

One of the other attackers punched Emma in retaliation, sending her reeling backward into the kitchen table. But she'd given Shea the opening she needed.

Shea scrambled across the floor toward her gun, her

injured arm useless but her determination unshaken. Darryl grabbed her ankle just as her fingers touched the weapon. "I'm going to enjoy killing you slow, Sheriff. You've caused me more trouble than any woman ever has."

A shot rang out, impossibly loud in the enclosed space. "The next one goes through your head, mister." Becky stood over them, her gun aimed directly at Darryl's skull. Her hands were steady now, maternal protectiveness overriding her natural pacifism. "Call off your men and get out of our cabin."

Annie and Deborah returned from the back of the house, dragging a man who was thoroughly tangled in fishing line and embedded hooks. He looked like he'd fought a giant spider and lost, blood seeping from dozens of small punctures.

"Stop where you are," Becky commanded, her voice carrying new authority. "I won't miss this time, and I promise you I mean it. Touch any of my friends again, and I'll kill you where you stand."

Darryl released Shea's ankle, his eyes fixed on the unwavering gun barrel pointed at his face. By the time she retrieved her weapon and regained her feet, he had signaled his men to retreat. They fled through the windows they'd entered, leaving their tangled comrade behind.

"This ain't over, Sheriff," Darryl snarled as he backed toward the door. "Not by a long shot. We'll be back, and next time we won't underestimate you ladies."

Shea got to her feet, swaying slightly from exhaustion and pain. "Everyone okay?"

Heads nodded around the room, though everyone bore evidence of the fight—cuts, bruises, torn clothing. But they were alive, and they'd proven they could fight back effectively.

Deborah and Annie immediately moved to push the bookcase back in front of the door, then slid the heavy kitchen table against it for additional reinforcement. The improvised barricade wouldn't stop a determined assault, but it would slow the next attack.

"Let's get this place secure again," Shea said, tucking her gun back into her waistband. "They won't come back unarmed next time. We've shown them we're dangerous—they'll respond accordingly."

The truth of that statement settled over the group like a heavy blanket. Their small victory had likely only made their situation more desperate.

"We need to move to the loft," Shea continued, her tactical mind already working through their next defensive position. "I doubt they'll try the deck approach again after what happened, and if we're higher than them, we can pick them off as they try to come up the stairs."

"Kill them, you mean." Becky's eyes widened with the realization of what survival was going to require. "I don't think I can do that. Not deliberately."

"Pretend your boys are here," Shea said gently but

firmly. "Think about them losing their mama because you couldn't do what was necessary to come home to them."

The suggestion hit its mark. Becky's expression hardened with maternal determination; there was nothing more dangerous than a mother protecting her children, even from a distance.

Shea went to the bedroom and removed the suitcases from under the bed in order to help their two wounded friends up to the loft. The hiding place had served its purpose, but now they needed all available fighters in their defensive position.

The loft wasn't ideal—there were no mattresses available for comfort, and although they'd have access to a small bathroom, there was no kitchen facility or refrigerator. But the elevated position was tactically sound.

"Bring up any weapons we have left, all the food and water, blankets—whatever will help us survive what's coming next," she instructed.

Rachel managed to climb the stairs by herself, though she moved slowly and carefully. Tessa leaned heavily on Shea, her wound making every step an ordeal.

"You should've seen that man when he ran into the fishing line," Tessa said with a weak grin as they climbed. "I could peek out through the suitcases and watch the whole thing. He started swinging his hands around like he'd walked through a spider web, but all he did was tangle himself more and drive the hooks deeper."

"Good, because the trap on the front door didn't work as planned." Darryl had found a way around that obstacle, probably by simply pushing through it with brute force. By the time she got Tessa settled in the loft, Shea's lungs were wheezing like those of a lifetime smoker.

She took two careful puffs from her inhaler, trying not to think about what would happen if she had a full-blown asthma attack. She hadn't brought a nebulizer machine, and she only had one extra inhaler in her backpack. Using the medication too frequently would eventually stop it from working effectively.

She lowered Tessa to the floor, then slid down the wall beside her, grateful for a moment's rest. The others carried up all the requested supplies—weapons, food, water, blankets, and even Shea's backpack.

Becky smiled down at her as she handed over the pack. "Thought you might need this."

"You are truly a marvel." Shea looked at each of her friends, memorizing their faces. "All of you are. If we don't make it home, I hope our families know how hard we fought to get back to them."

There had been moments of despair and crippling fear throughout their ordeal, but their faces now held a steely resolve that hadn't been there when they'd arrived for their weekend getaway. They wouldn't go down easily.

A cry for help from outside interrupted her thoughts. Shea stood and moved to the loft window, raising it carefully. Below them, one of Darryl's men lay impaled on the glass shards she'd embedded in the tree branch, his body twisted at an unnatural angle.

"What do we do with him?" Annie joined her at the window, handing her a water bottle.

"I'm not sure yet. Leave him there for now. His buddies seem to have abandoned him." The man might be too seriously injured to get down on his own, but he also wasn't an immediate threat to the women.

Shea twisted the cap off the bottle and took a long drink. "How much water do we have left?"

"Enough for each of us to have three bottles a day for the next two days," Annie reported. "You know Becky—she always brings extra supplies."

"Thank God for that." She took another swig, then set the bottle on the window ledge.

The injured man below glared up at them despite the obvious pain etched across his features. "I'm impaled here, you wretched women! I'm bleeding to death."

Shea shrugged unsympathetically. "Guess you need to unimpale yourself then."

He called her a string of unflattering names that would have made a truck driver blush. "Darryl is going to sacrifice all of you to the old gods. You're just delaying the inevitable."

"I don't think so." She withdrew from the window,

but the man's words echoed in her mind. They couldn't just leave him there to die, despite what he and his friends had done. She wasn't that kind of person. While she could kill in self-defense when lives were at stake, she couldn't simply watch an unarmed, wounded man bleed to death.

But what could they do with him? He wasn't a rabid animal they could simply put it out of its misery.

She was too tired to think clearly, the constant stress and physical demands of their situation taking their toll. She finished the water and turned to her friends. "What do y'all want to do with that man down there?"

"Leave him there to rot," Deborah said flatly, holding a water bottle to a growing bruise on her forehead. "Someone hit me during the fight, and I'm not feeling particularly charitable toward any of them."

Emma closed her eyes and leaned her head back against the loft wall. "I honestly don't care anymore. I'm too tired to think about mercy."

"What do you want to do?" Becky asked. "You know I can't be part of killing anyone, even them."

"I can't kill an unarmed, wounded man either," Shea admitted with a heavy exhale. "But what if we brought him up here, tied him up securely, and interrogated him? He might give us information that would help us escape or survive until help arrives."

"Or he'll kill us in our sleep when we let our guard down," Annie pointed out practically.

"I don't think he's in any condition to pose that kind

of threat. Look at him—he can barely move."

Annie planted her fists on her hips. "How exactly do you propose getting him up here? He's impaled on a tree branch twenty feet below us."

"We'll have to lower something and pull him up." Shea peered over the loft railing at the main floor below. Some of the rope they'd used for their improvised traps lay coiled in a corner. It might be strong enough to haul him inside, and then they could tie him up securely.

She prayed she wasn't making a grave mistake that would cost them all their lives.

"Let me and Deborah handle the rope work," Annie said. "You can't pull him up with one good arm. I know you put up an incredible fight down there, but you need to let us do what we can. We can't have you collapsing on us when we need you most."

"Thank you. I'll get the rope." She could hold her weapon on the man while they hauled him inside, ensuring he couldn't cause trouble during the rescue.

Before any of them could object or change their minds, she made her way carefully down the stairs. Rope in hand, she paused at the bottom and stared back up at the loft. The wooden steps were the only way to reach their elevated position—a natural chokepoint that could work in their favor.

Hopefully, she could keep Darryl's men from reaching the stairs when they returned for their final assault. A few more strategically placed traps might help even the odds.

And they would come again, probably before dawn. Of that she had absolutely no doubt. This had been just a probing attack, a test of their defenses and capabilities.

The next assault would be their last stand, one way or another.

Chapter Nine

Back upstairs, Shea formed the rope into a noose with practiced efficiency, her law enforcement training having included basic knotwork. She leaned out the window, assessing the injured man's position on the glass-studded branch below. "I'm going to toss you a rope. Grab hold and we'll drag you inside."

The man's eyes widened with a mixture of pain and disbelief. "Are you crazy? I'm already sliced up from all this glass. Pulling me across those shards will shred me like cabbage through a grater."

"Well, you can stay there if you want." Shea shrugged with apparent indifference, though inside she felt the familiar conflict between her humanitarian instincts and the harsh realities of survival. "Makes no difference to me."

"Wait, wait, wait!" His voice cracked with desperation as she started to withdraw from the window.

She leaned back out, projecting more patience than

she felt. "Change your mind?"

"You're a sick woman, but toss me the damn rope." His voice carried a tone of resignation, mixed with grudging respect for her tactical position.

Shea threw the looped rope with careful aim. The noose landed inches from his outstretched hand, close enough for him to grab despite his compromised position.

The man looped it around his wrist with shaking fingers, then tried crawling forward along the branch. "I can't do it. The glass is cutting me to pieces."

"I'm glad to help." Shea motioned for Deborah to join her, and they both gripped the rope. "On three. One, two, three."

They tugged with coordinated effort, and the man screamed as they dragged him across the embedded glass shards. Each inch of progress left a trail of blood and torn fabric behind him. When he finally reached the window, he fell inside the loft in a heap, several pieces of glass still embedded in his clothing and exposed skin.

Under different circumstances, Shea might have felt sorry for him. As it was, she could care less about his pain, but as a human being with a badge and an oath, she had to offer some basic medical attention. "Becky, tend to his cuts the best you can."

While Becky reluctantly moved to help their prisoner, Shea jerked the man's hands behind him and secured them with the same rope she'd used to pull him inside. She made sure the knots were tight enough to prevent escape but not so tight as to cut off circulation entirely.

A twig snapped somewhere outside, the sound sharp in the relative quiet. Shea jerked upright, every nerve suddenly alert. When no further sound came, she decided to head back downstairs to complete her defensive preparations. Once all the women were safely settled in the loft, she planned to set a few more trip wires to prevent easy access for anyone else.

The improvised traps would be simple yet effective—when triggered, the wires would shoot nails into the ankles and legs of anyone attempting to climb the stairs. It might not stop a determined assault, but it would definitely slow them down and give the women a crucial advantage. She also wanted to gather anything in the loft that could be used as a weapon against attackers—books, bottles, or anything heavy enough to cause damage or distraction.

After setting the new traps with meticulous care, she returned to their hostage. She sat on the small bench at the end of one of the beds and studied him with the dispassionate gaze of an interrogator. Blood had saturated the torn flannel shirt he wore, but Becky had managed to patch up the worst of his cuts with strips of torn bedsheet. The man wasn't in danger of anything more serious than possible infection.

His dark eyes bore into hers with undisguised hatred. "What do you want?" Spittle clung to the scraggly end of his unkempt beard. "If you think tying me up and keeping me as a hostage is gonna help you get out of here alive, you're completely delusional. You're already dead, all of you. You just don't know it yet."

Shea remained outwardly calm, though her voice carried a steely edge that hadn't been there when she'd first arrived at the cabin. "Why are you doing this? You've been terrorizing us since the first night. What do you and your friends get out of hunting innocent people?"

The man laughed, the sound bitter and cruel, echoing off the loft's slanted walls. "Don't take it personal, Sheriff. You're simply prey, nothing more. Like a deer or a rabbit during hunting season."

She saw the absolute truth in his eyes and realized he meant every word. To him and his companions, she and her friends weren't human beings with families, dreams, and futures—they were just animals to be hunted for sport. The casual cruelty of it took her breath away.

Well, it had become personal to her now. She pulled her knife from her pocket and opened the blade with deliberate slowness, setting it on her knee where he could see it clearly.

The man's gaze flicked to the weapon, then to the women surrounding him, then to Tessa and Rachel lying wounded on makeshift beds. For the first time since they'd captured him, the bravado faded from his weathered face. His confident grin slipped.

"It's just a game, you understand?" His voice had quieted, losing some of its earlier arrogance. "A thrill for us city boys who spend most of our time behind desks. We bought this place a few years back, kept it maintained nice so folks would want to rent it. We watch and wait until someone books the cabin, then we have ourselves some real hunting. City slickers are easy targets, you see. Out here in the middle of nowhere, no one will come to help you."

"That's where you're wrong." It was Shea's turn to smile, and the expression was far from pleasant. "One of us made it out. She's probably down the mountain by now, calling for help. Rescue teams will be here soon. So, what's your endgame? You, for one, won't be walking away from this. I've already killed two of your friends. What's one more corpse to add to the pile?"

He shrugged with affected nonchalance, though she could see fear beginning to creep into his expression. "There's enough of us left. We'll finish you off before any alleged help arrives. Even if someone is coming, they won't get here in time."

Dread settled over the women like a heavy blanket. Shea had suspected they were nothing more than entertainment for these predators, but hearing the man speak so callously about killing them sent ice through her veins. Ice that was already beginning to melt as fire started to rage inside her chest.

How could they use this man to their advantage?

She doubted his leader would care much whether this particular follower lived or died. Men like that saw their subordinates as expendable resources, nothing more. Losing team members would be another part of the game to someone that ruthless.

She'd encountered men like their leader before in her law enforcement career. What mattered most to them was winning, maintaining control, and proving their dominance. Their followers were nothing more than collateral damage in the service of their ego.

The bound man began to fidget under her steady gaze, clearly uncomfortable with the intensity of her stare. "Can I get some water? I'm bleeding and dehydrated."

"No. We're running short as it is. We won't waste our limited food or water on you." She pushed to her feet with deliberate slowness, her movements calculated to project menace.

The rumble of approaching engines from outside caused her to break into a cold sweat. Multiple vehicles, moving fast, heading directly for the cabin. She closed her knife and slipped it back into her pocket, then grabbed her gun and checked the ammunition. "They're coming back. Everyone get ready."

"What about him?" Annie asked, clutching the fireplace poker like a weapon.

"Leave him where he is. He's not going anywhere, and he might be useful as a bargaining chip." Though privately, Shea doubted his companions would care enough about his welfare to negotiate.

The cabin shuddered under a renewed onslaught of objects being hurled against the outside walls. Rocks, bottles, pieces of lumber—anything heavy enough to make noise and cause psychological pressure. Loud country music blared from multiple speakers, the volume cranked high enough to vibrate the windows and hide any sounds the attackers would make as they positioned themselves around the building.

"Aim carefully when you throw things," Shea warned her friends, raising her voice to be heard over the musical assault. "We can't retrieve anything once it's thrown, so make every projectile count. Pile up whatever you can near the railing. Anything big enough to use as a shield, position it in front of the wounded for cover."

Her friends sprang into action with the efficiency born of desperation and hard experience. They'd learned to work together under pressure, each woman knowing her role in their desperate defense.

Suddenly, the music stopped with jarring abruptness. The silence that followed was almost as bad as the noise had been, filled with ominous potential. Heavy footsteps sounded on the cabin's main floor, multiple sets moving with military precision.

"Sheriff?" The voice that called up carried casual confidence, as if this was nothing more than a social visit.

"What can I help you with?" Shea called back, releasing the safety on her gun and positioning herself behind the most substantial cover available.

"They've got me tied up, boss!" Their prisoner struggled against his bindings with renewed desperation. "I'm hurt real bad up here. They dragged me across glass!"

The man below seemed to care not at all about his subordinate's welfare. "We're going to come up there, Sheriff, and take all you ladies out to our special clearing in the woods. It won't be pleasant for you, but it won't last very long either. Time for this game to end—I've got to get back to my family for Sunday dinner."

The casual mention of family while planning their murders was perhaps the most chilling thing Shea had heard yet. This man led a double life, returning home to play the role of a loving husband and father after spending his weekends hunting humans for sport.

"That sounds like a personal problem to me," Shea replied, fighting to keep her voice steady.

"Have it your way then." The voice below carried a tone of resignation tinged with anticipation. "Boys, they want to do this the hard way. Go get them."

With a nod that Shea couldn't see but could hear in the sudden increase of activity, multiple men headed for the stairs. The first one screamed as her improvised nail traps embedded metal spikes into his lower legs. His agonized cry was cut short as he tumbled backward down the stairs.

With a curse that echoed through the cabin, the

second man tried to rush past his fallen comrade, only to receive the same treatment from another concealed trap. As they writhed on the stairs in obvious pain, three more men pushed past them with grim determination.

Pandemonium broke out as the women threw everything they had gathered. Books, bottles, candlesticks, picture frames—a rain of improvised missiles filled the stairwell. The attacking men dodged what they could and absorbed what they couldn't, pressing forward despite the barrage.

Annie scored a direct hit with the fireplace poker, the heavy iron tool laying one attacker's cheek open to the bone. He stumbled backward with a howl of pain, rolling down the stairs and taking the two wounded men with him in a tangle of limbs and curses. That left only two more attackers, plus their leader, to deal with.

The remaining two men reached the top of the stairs with guns drawn, their faces grim with professional determination.

"Come on down, Sheriff, and my men won't shoot your friends," the voice from below called out with false reasonableness. "Just you and me, one-on-one. A fair fight to the death, winner take all. What do you say?"

Shea peered carefully over the railing, trying to get a visual on their tormentor. "You're not Darryl."

"Never said I was. You made that assumption based on our earlier conversation. I'm his younger brother, Bruce. Darryl had some family business he had to take care of, so he asked me to finish this job for him."

The casual way he discussed murder as a "job" sent fresh chills through Shea's system. These people had turned killing into a family business, passed down through generations like any other trade.

The two gunmen who had made it to the loft level aimed their weapons directly at Tessa and Rachel, lying helpless on their makeshift beds. The threat was unmistakable—refuse the challenge and watch her wounded friends die.

Shea had no choice, and they all knew it. She had to fight, had to trust that this Bruce had enough twisted honor to keep his word. "I'm coming down." With a deep breath that might be her last, she handed her gun to Deborah, then withdrew her knife. "If I win, everyone goes free. Tell your men."

Bruce laughed, the sound carrying genuine amusement. "You heard her, boys. They can all walk away if she manages to best me in single combat."

The words carried the weight of a binding agreement, though Shea wondered how much the promise of a dead man would be worth.

This would not be a civilized fight like the sparring matches she'd participated in during her kickboxing training. This would be a primal battle for survival, with no rules and no referee except death itself.

"If I win, we go free," she repeated as she descended the stairs, wanting the terms established in front of witnesses.

"Absolutely," Bruce agreed with a grin that revealed missing teeth. "A deal's a deal."

The large man was waiting for her at the bottom of the stairs, and he charged without warning the moment her feet touched the main floor. Shea barely had time to dodge his first wild swing, countering with a roundhouse kick to his substantial gut.

He bellowed like an enraged bull and came at her again, using his superior size and weight to try to overwhelm her. Grabbing her around the waist, he slammed her into the nearest wall hard enough to drive the air from her lungs.

Shea rolled to the side, using his momentum against him, and managed to take them both outside onto the cabin's front porch. The larger man slipped on loose pebbles and pine needles but quickly regained his balance with the sure-footedness of someone accustomed to outdoor violence.

He pulled a wicked-looking knife from his belt, the blade longer and heavier than her own. "I'm going to gut you like a fish, little lady. Been looking forward to this all week."

Shea bared her teeth in a feral grin that matched his own. "You can try." She slashed out with her weapon, the blade catching him across the ribcage and opening a line of red through his shirt. Blood spurted, making her hand slippery, but the wound wasn't deep enough to slow him down significantly.

The fight continued with brutal intensity, each combatant looking for an opening to deliver a killing blow. Bruce was stronger and had longer reach, but Shea was faster and better trained. Soon, exhaustion threatened to slow her down as the accumulated damage from days of violence took its toll. Every one of his hits that connected made her weaker, and a particularly vicious blow to her injured arm made her cry out despite her efforts to stay silent.

She blinked back tears of pain and frustration. She couldn't lose this fight—her friends' lives depended on her victory, and failure meant death for all of them.

"What's the matter, girlie? Am I wearing you down?" Bruce gave a shark-like grin as he circled her like a predator. "I can do this all day. I've got the stamina of a man half my age."

One more jab, one more thrust, one more kick—Shea kept her eye on the ultimate prize, taking grim satisfaction when another calculated stab caught him across the forearm and made him drop his knife. She immediately kicked the weapon out of his reach, then began circling him like the prey he'd suddenly become.

The tables had turned, and now she was the hunter.

Rage darkened Bruce's weathered face as Shea stayed just outside his reach, forcing him to come to her on her terms. "Stop dancing around and let's finish this like adults!"

Shea shook her head and made a beckoning motion with her fingers, taunting him into making mistakes.

His gaze flicked nervously to the knife in her hand, suddenly realizing that his size advantage meant nothing against a sharp blade wielded by someone who knew how to use it.

"What's the matter, Bruce? Can't you take down one little woman?" She grinned with predatory satisfaction.

The psychological warfare worked precisely as intended. She didn't see the desperate punch coming until it was too late. He smashed her lip against her teeth with enough force to split the skin, pushing her backward across the uneven ground. She slipped on a patch of pine needles and almost fell, only fierce determination and years of balance training keeping her upright.

She wanted this fight to be over as much as he did, but she also wanted to win.

The other women, minus Tessa and Rachel, who were too wounded to move, now watched from the porch like spectators at some twisted gladiatorial contest. All of the remaining attackers, including the one she'd tied up earlier, had weapons aimed at her friends' heads. She had no real guarantee they'd be allowed to leave even if she won the fight, but losing would definitely result in all their deaths.

She could only pray that Bruce had retained some vestige of honor despite his profession.

He threw another punch, this one going wide as fatigue affected his accuracy. Seeing her opportunity,

Shea ducked under his extended arm and drove her elbow into his temple with all the force she could muster, disorienting him.

With a roar of desperate fury, she tackled him to the ground, using gravity and leverage to overcome his size advantage.

His breath left him in a harsh whoosh as they hit the earth. His eyes widened in surprise at the first stab to his chest, then shock as she struck again and again, until the light finally faded from his eyes and he lay still beneath her.

Shea wiped her bloody knife on his shirt and turned to face the remaining men, swaying slightly from exhaustion and blood loss. "Go. Leave us alone. He said we'd be free if I won, and he's dead, so that means I won fair and square."

The surviving attackers exchanged uncertain glances, clearly unsure how to proceed without their leader's guidance. After a long moment of tense silence, one of them climbed into the driver's seat of the nearest truck.

"This isn't the end of this," he called out as the engines started. "Darryl won't take kindly to you killing his baby brother. He'll be coming for you."

"Too bad for Darryl," Shea replied, though the threat sent ice through her veins.

It took every ounce of strength she had left to remain upright until the trucks disappeared down the mountain road. Only when she was sure they were gone did she allow herself to collapse onto the cabin's front step, her body finally acknowledging the accumulated damage from days of fighting.

"Get whatever food and water we have left," she gasped to her friends. "Grab your warmest jackets and help Tessa and Rachel down the stairs. We're leaving this place right now."

"You're in no condition to travel—" Becky started to protest, her maternal instincts kicking in.

"You heard what that man said. Darryl will be coming to avenge his brother, and when he gets here, he won't be interested in games or single combat." Shea took a deep, shuddering breath and glanced down at her blood-soaked clothing. "We have to be long gone by then."

She forced herself to stand on trembling legs. "Also, tie up those wounded men we left on the stairs and drag Bruce's body inside the cabin. Let's not leave any evidence of what happened here."

Inside the bathroom, she cleaned up as best she could with the limited time available, washing Bruce's blood from her hands and face before changing into clean leggings and the ridiculous pink T-shirt she'd been avoiding. They were going to shine like beacons in the dark forest, making them easy targets for anyone tracking them.

Wait—she'd forgotten about her black hoodie. The dark fabric would hide the pink and provide some camouflage. She instructed the others to wear their darkest clothing and cover their hair if possible.

"We're really getting out of here?" Hope shined in Emma's exhausted eyes for the first time in days.

"Yes, we're leaving right now."

"What if Kara comes back with help? What if she's trying to find us?"

"If she returns with law enforcement, they'll be able to track our path down the mountain." Shea hoped that was true. "If we have someone skilled at reading signs, they'll be able to determine which direction we went."

Eight women, two of them seriously wounded, wouldn't be able to move quickly through difficult terrain. But staying at the cabin meant certain death when Darryl arrived.

Becky handed her a lightweight backpack, its contents carefully chosen. "The rest of us will carry the food and water supplies. All that's in yours are your extra ammunition and your backup gun."

"Thank you." Shea didn't think she'd be able to carry much additional weight. She wasn't sure how far she'd be able to travel as things stood.

Summoning what little energy she had left, she headed for the tree line with her gun ready, her friends following close behind in a protective formation around their wounded companions.

Behind them, the cabin sat empty and blood-stained, a monument to their survival and their refusal to become victims.

Ahead lay the dark forest and an uncertain future, but at least they were moving toward safety instead of waiting for death to find them.

Chapter Ten

A cold autumn rain started to fall, the droplets cutting through the forest canopy like icy needles. Becky mumbled something about how the weather forecast had predicted a storm, but she'd thought the women would be safely heading home when it hit. The irony wasn't lost on any of them—they'd planned to be packing up their memories of a perfect girls' weekend, not fleeing for their lives through hostile wilderness.

"What about Melanie?" Emma asked, shoving her wet hair out of her face with trembling hands. "We just left her there in that cabin."

The question hit Shea like a physical blow, adding guilt to the already overwhelming burden of responsibility she carried. "We had no choice." Her voice was rougher than she intended, emotion threatening to break through her carefully maintained composure. She glanced over her shoulder to check on their progress. Becky supported Tessa on one side while Deborah helped Rachel maintain her footing on the other. "It's all we can do to get ourselves out of these woods alive."

The truth was harsh but undeniable. They were struggling through unfamiliar territory, the same wilderness where she'd sent Kara days ago and from which her friend had yet to return. The weight of command pressed down on her shoulders like a lead blanket—every decision she made could mean the difference between life and death for all of them.

The burden of having killed three men in the span of a few days dogged her steps with every labored breath. The faces of the dead men flashed through her mind unbidden—their expressions in the moment before life left their eyes, the weight of their bodies as they fell. She'd never taken a life before this nightmare began, and now she was a killer three times over. The knowledge sat in her stomach like a stone, cold and indigestible.

Worse was the gnawing worry that she didn't have the strength left to get her friends to safety. Her body was running on fumes and sheer willpower, every muscle screaming in protest with each step. The accumulated damage from days of violence and stress was taking its toll, and she wasn't sure how much longer she could maintain the pace their survival demanded.

How long until Darryl started tracking them? It wouldn't be challenging to follow the obvious trail they were leaving behind—eight exhausted women stumbling through the forest weren't exactly masters of stealth. Despite the cold that was already seeping into her bones, Shea found herself wishing for a torrential downpour that would wash away any signs of their passage.

Becky yelped behind her, the sound sharp with pain and surprise.

Shea spun around to see her friend stumbling, her supporting arm slipping away from Tessa as she fought to regain her balance. Both women went down in a tangle of limbs and exhausted gasps. "Let's rest," Shea decided, though every instinct screamed at her to keep moving. As much as she dreaded stopping, they couldn't maintain even this moderate pace. Not even she could, and her friends were in far worse shape.

With expressions of profound relief, everyone stopped and collapsed where they stood, seemingly unmindful of the rain that was soaking through their clothes and the mud that was seeping through the fabric. Shea did the same, using the substantial trunk of an old oak tree for support. Her legs felt like rubber, shaking with exhaustion and adrenaline crash.

The far-off rumble of an engine from the road leading to the cabin reached her ears through the patter of rain, alerting her to the fact that they hadn't traveled nearly far enough from the scene of their escape. The sound was distant but unmistakable vehicles moving fast, heading toward the cabin where they'd left Bruce's body and his wounded men.

It wouldn't take Darryl long to find his dead brother and free his injured followers. Then the real hunt would begin, and this time there would be no games, no psychological warfare, no single combat. This time it would be pure vengeance, swift and brutal.

She struggled to her feet, ignoring the protests from every joint and muscle. "Time to go."

Groans and grumbling filled the air, but her friends somehow found the strength to stand. Emma shook her head in disbelief, rainwater dripping from her bedraggled hair. "How can you keep going like this? I'm not even injured, and I feel like I'm running on empty."

"If we don't keep moving, we die." The simple truth cut through any complaints or self-pity. Shea refused to let them die on this mountain because of a group of evil men who saw murder as entertainment. "That's the only choice we have—move or die."

"Like Kara," Emma murmured, the words barely audible above the sound of falling rain.

"We don't know that Kara is dead." Shea's voice carried more conviction than she felt. "Until someone finds a body, I'm going to hold onto hope. The chance that she got lost is just as strong as the possibility that she was caught."

But even as she said it, doubt gnawed at her. Kara had been gone for days now, long enough to reach the gas station and summon help if she'd made it safely down the mountain. The fact that no rescue had materialized suggested that either she'd never reached civilization or her calls for help had been ignored or misunderstood.

After another grueling hour of stumbling through increasingly rugged terrain, the rain increased dramatically, transforming from steady drops to a punishing downpour that made visibility nearly impossible. Shea led the group to a rocky overhang near a rushing creek, the only shelter they'd seen in miles.

The women squeezed into the inadequate space, huddling together for warmth like refugees from some ancient catastrophe. Each labored breath created visible clouds in the increasingly cold air, and Shea could see hypothermia becoming a real concern if they had to stay exposed much longer.

Every crack of a branch or rustle of leaves felt amplified in the confined space, setting everyone's already frayed nerves further on edge. Shea glanced around at the terror etched on each of her friends' faces, wishing desperately that she could offer some comfort or reassurance. But empty platitudes would help no one and lies would only make things worse when reality inevitably intruded.

"We can't stay here long," Annie whispered, her voice barely audible above the sound of rushing water. "They'll catch up to us eventually."

Shea nodded grimly. "I'm hoping they'll wait for the rain to let up before continuing their search. That should help maintain our head start." She studied the creek that rushed past their hiding place. "We'll use the water to hide our tracks. Moving in the creek will make it much harder for them to follow us."

And if they were fortunate, none of them would succumb to hypothermia in the process.

A dog barked somewhere in the distance, the sound cutting through the storm like a knife. Then another joined it, and another. The baying was unmistakable—hunting hounds on a scent trail.

Darryl had brought tracking dogs to find them.

"We've got to go right now." Shea bolted to her feet, shoving aside the pain that shot through her injured arm and the exhaustion that made every movement feel like swimming through molasses. "As fast as we can manage."

Without waiting for a response, she splashed into the creek, gasping as the ice-cold water shocked her already abused system. The current was stronger than it appeared, threatening to sweep her feet out from under her with each step.

She had no clear idea which direction would lead them to the road, but she had to make a choice. Think! Had the creek crossed under the mountain road on their way up? Had they driven over a bridge? Yes, she remembered now—there had been a small bridge near the bottom of the mountain.

She turned right, following the current downstream. The creek should eventually lead them to the road that wound up the mountain. From there, they could stay hidden in the tree line until they reached the gas station, where help might be waiting.

It would work. It had to work because the alternative was death.

She held back to help Becky support Tessa while Annie took over assisting Rachel. The creek bed was treacherous, covered with moss-slicked rocks that threatened to send them tumbling with every step. Shea's feet quickly went numb from the frigid water, making it even harder to maintain her footing.

Emma went down with a shriek that echoed off the surrounding trees, disappearing beneath the surface for a terrifying moment before Lauren hauled her back to her feet. The fall had soaked her completely, and Shea could see her lips already beginning to turn blue from the cold.

The bark of a tracking dog sounded much closer now, joined by the distant shouts of men coordinating their search. Darryl was finally getting the type of hunt he'd always wanted—desperate prey fleeing through hostile wilderness with nowhere to hide.

The women had truly become the hunted animals their tormentors saw them as.

Seconds crawled by like hours. Minutes stretched into what felt like an eternity of cold, fear, and exhaustion. The rain finally began to let up after what her watch told her was another full hour, though it felt like they'd been struggling through the creek for days. Clouds parted to reveal a full moon hanging like a spotlight in the blue-velvet sky.

"I've got to stop," Tessa gasped, her face gray with pain and exhaustion. She gagged, then retched into the rushing water, her body finally rebelling against the abuse it had endured.

"We can't stop here. The dogs will pick up our scent if we stay in one place too long." Shea cast a worried look behind them, scanning the forest for any sign of pursuit. She continued forward until she found a spot on the opposite bank where tree roots and erosion had created a natural ladder they could use to climb out of the water.

Grasping a thick root that protruded from the muddy bank, she pulled herself up with her one good arm, then turned to help the others. Each woman who emerged from the creek was shaking uncontrollably, their wet clothes clinging to a body that was already showing signs of hypothermia.

"We follow the creek until it meets the road, then take the road down to the gas station where we can call for help," she explained, though her own voice was beginning to shake from the cold.

"Any idea how far that might be?" Becky asked, grasping Shea's offered hand with fingers that felt like ice.

"No, I'm completely turned around at this point." The admission was hard to make, but honesty was more important than false confidence. "For all I know, we could have circled back toward the cabin. But we're bound to hit the road eventually if we keep following the water downstream."

"Sheriff!" The shout echoed through the forest, much closer than she'd expected.

She spun toward the sound, trying to pinpoint its origin through the maze of trees and shadows. The pursuers weren't directly on their heels yet, but they were definitely gaining ground with the help of their tracking dogs.

"You can run all you want, but you won't get away from me!" Darryl's voice carried clearly through the night air, filled with the confidence of a predator who knew his prey was weakening. "When I catch up to you—and I will catch up—I'm going to make you squeal before I let you die."

Of that threat, Shea had absolutely no doubt. She'd killed his brother in single combat, humiliated his men, and cost him his perfect hunting ground. When he finally cornered them, the vengeance would be creative and prolonged.

She increased their pace as much as their battered bodies could manage, though she could see that several of her friends were approaching the absolute limits of their endurance. They could rest when they were safe, or when they were dead—those were the only two options available.

Shivering uncontrollably now, she shoved aside a low-hanging branch that scratched at her face, then pushed through a section of thick brush that seemed to claw at their clothes with thorny fingers. From the crashing sounds behind her, she knew the others were following, though she could hear the labored breathing and occasional whimpered curses that spoke of their deteriorating condition.

She wanted desperately to offer hope and encouragement, some words that would give her friends the strength to continue. But it took every ounce of energy she possessed just to keep putting one foot in front of the other. Speaking would require breath she couldn't spare and concentration she needed for navigation.

The tracking dogs were getting closer—she could hear them clearly now, their excited baying indicating they'd found a strong scent trail. Behind the dogs came the voices of their handlers, coordinating the search with military precision.

"This way! They came through here!"

"Dogs have something! Moving northeast along the creek!"

"Spread out! Don't let them slip through!"

The professional efficiency of their pursuit was terrifying. These weren't random sadists playing games—they were experienced hunters who knew exactly what they were doing.

Shea pushed through the last section of dense undergrowth and suddenly stepped onto smooth asphalt, the transition so abrupt that she stumbled and nearly fell. They'd found the road, but in her exhaustion and disorientation, she'd emerged directly into the path of oncoming traffic.

A horn blared like the trumpet of judgment as a large vehicle swerved violently to avoid hitting her. Headlights swept across the group of bedraggled women like searchlights, illuminating their desperate condition for a split second before the driver fought to regain control.

The combination of relief, exhaustion, and delayed shock finally overwhelmed Shea's system. Her legs gave out completely, and she crumpled into the muddy ditch beside the road, her body finally surrendering to the accumulated trauma of the past few days.

As consciousness faded around the edges, she heard car doors slamming and voices calling out—whether friend or foe, she couldn't tell. But they'd made it to the road, which meant they'd made it far enough for help to find them.

Whether that help would arrive in time remained to be seen.

Chapter Eleven

A man in a worn cowboy hat and crisp sheriff's uniform rushed toward her, his boots splashing through the muddy ditch. "Ma'am? Can you hear me?"

Shea held up a trembling hand for him to help her, her voice hoarse from exhaustion and exposure. "Nice to finally meet you in person, Sheriff Westbrook."

"Sheriff Callahan?" He helped her to her feet with gentle but firm hands, his handsome face creasing with concern as the other bedraggled women emerged from the woods like ghosts materialized from a nightmare. "Good Lord, what happened up there? We got a call from some campers about a woman asking for help, but we had no idea—"

Another vehicle pulled up with flashing lights, and Kara climbed out of the back seat, her face streaked with tears of relief. "Shea! Thank God you made it."

"You made it." Tears blurred Shea's vision as the reality of rescue finally sank in. Her friend was alive, unharmed, and help had come. After days of hoping against hope, the cavalry had finally arrived.

"After wandering around lost for what felt like forever, I stumbled across some weekend campers about fifteen miles down the mountain." Kara wrapped Shea in a careful hug, mindful of her obvious injuries. "You girls have been through absolute hell from the looks of things."

Sheriff Westbrook's radio crackled with updates from his deputies. "Your friend told us some locals have harassed you? She said one of your group was killed?" His experienced eyes swept over the group, automatically cataloging injuries and assessing their condition.

"Yes, and they're still after us." As if summoned by her words, a tracking dog barked somewhere in the forest behind them, causing her to flinch involuntarily. "They have dogs. They've been hunting us like animals."

By now, four sheriff's department vehicles had pulled up, their red and blue lights casting a strobing glow over the scene. Sheriff Westbrook immediately ordered his deputies to spread out and round up the men who were pursuing the women, his voice carrying the authority of someone accustomed to dangerous situations.

"Ladies, I need you all to wait in the squad cars until the ambulances arrive," he said, gesturing toward the vehicles. "You'll be safe there, and you need medical attention."

The women didn't have to be told twice. Getting out of the exposed woods and into the warmth of the patrol cars sounded like paradise to Shea's ears. Darryl and his hunting party were no longer her immediate concern—that burden could finally shift to people trained and equipped to handle it.

She climbed into the back seat of the sheriff's cruiser and closed her eyes, feeling the accumulated stress of the past few days beginning to catch up with her. The hours to come would undoubtedly be filled with endless questions, reports, and medical examinations, but for the first time since this nightmare began, she could actually envision surviving to see them.

Her lungs suddenly constricted with a familiar wheeze, the stress and cold finally triggering the asthma attack she'd been fighting off for hours. She opened her eyes and frantically fished in her backpack for her emergency inhaler. One puff, two... but instead of relief, her breathing became even more constricted.

Panic setting in, she pounded on the patrol car window to get Becky's attention. "Can't breathe," she managed to gasp out between labored attempts to draw air.

Her friend immediately understood the crisis and raced toward the arriving ambulance, waving her arms to get the paramedics' attention. Within minutes, Shea had a portable nebulizer machine pressed to her mouth, the familiar medication finally opening her airways enough for her to speak.

"Tend to my friends first," she said around the mouthpiece, her voice muffled but determined. "I'll be fine now that I can breathe."

Now that rescue had arrived and the sheriff's department was taking care of Darryl and his men, her adrenaline finally began to ebb. Without the constant surge of fight-or-flight hormones keeping her upright, her traitorous body began to succumb to the cumulative effects of her wounds and the psychological trauma of the past few days. For the first time since Melanie's murder, Shea no longer had to be the strong one, the protector, the one with all the answers.

When the paramedic returned to check her breathing and examine her injuries, he insisted on loading her into the ambulance despite her half-hearted protests. "We've got good people taking care of your friends, ma'am. But I need to take a proper look at these wounds. We'll be driving to the regional hospital in Langley. You might as well accept the fact that you're coming with us whether you like it or not."

"My deputies can handle the situation from here," Sheriff Westbrook assured her, appearing at the ambulance doors. "I'll come to the hospital when we've finished processing the scene to ask you some official questions. You're in excellent hands with these folks."

"I want to see this through to the end," Shea protested weakly, though she knew she was in no condition to be of any help.

"I'm sorry, but that's not going to happen. You're not officially acting sheriff yet, Callahan." His tone was gentle but firm. "See you at the hospital." He clapped a supportive hand on the side of the ambulance. "She's all yours, boys."

"What about the others?" Shea asked as the paramedic began checking her vital signs.

"They'll all be brought to Langley for evaluation. I want everyone checked over thoroughly, not just those with visible wounds." Westbrook turned and headed back toward the edge of the woods, reaching for his service weapon as the sound of gunfire erupted from the forest. "Get these women out of here right now!"

Sirens blaring, three crowded ambulances sped away from the chaotic scene, carrying the survivors toward safety and medical care.

Shea glanced around the ambulance to where Becky and Deborah sat with shell-shocked expressions, their faces pale but determined. Each ambulance carried one seriously injured woman plus several others who needed evaluation and treatment.

Kara sniffed, having insisted on riding along rather than staying behind. "I'm so sorry it took me so long to get help to you. If I hadn't gotten lost in those damned woods—"

"It's okay," Shea interrupted, stretching out her uninjured arm from the gurney to comfort her friend. "We all got lost up there. That mountain is like a maze."

"If I'd gotten help sooner, maybe Melanie would still be alive. Maybe you and Tessa and Rachel wouldn't be hurt so badly." The guilt in Kara's voice was unmistakable.

"Maybe, maybe not." Shea gripped her friend's hand tightly. "What matters is that you made it out alive and brought help. We were starting to think you were dead, and that fear was almost as bad as everything else we went through."

"Do you think those men will be caught?" Kara asked, glancing nervously out the ambulance windows as if expecting pursuit.

"Yes," Shea replied with confidence she actually felt. "Sheriff Westbrook knows what he's doing."

Again, unexpected remorse over having killed three men swept through her consciousness like a dark tide. She hadn't had any real choice in the matter—it had been kill or be killed, with her friends' lives hanging in the balance. But taking human lives still left a stain on her soul that she wasn't sure would ever thoroughly wash clean. She might be in law enforcement, but she'd never imagined she'd have to kill anyone in the line of duty.

At the hospital, the wounded were immediately taken in one direction while the others were led to a separate area for evaluation. Panic rippled through Shea at the prospect of being separated from her friends. After what they'd all been through together, she wanted and needed them around her for psychological comfort as much as anything else.

"You'll be just fine, honey," a middle-aged nurse assured her, patting her shoulder with practiced compassion. "Some antibiotics, proper stitches, and rest will have you back on your feet in no time."

"What about Rachel and Tessa? How badly are they hurt?"

"I don't have information about your friends right now, but you're my immediate concern." The nurse began preparing supplies for wound care. "I'll make sure the doctors keep you updated on their conditions, I promise."

She'd have to settle for that reassurance. Shea closed her eyes, finally allowing exhaustion to claim her. When she woke sometime later, a doctor she didn't recognize was leaning over her bed, studying her chart.

"How long was I unconscious?" she asked, struggling to orient herself.

"A couple of hours," he replied with what seemed like a genuine smile. "We cleaned and properly dressed your wounds, gave you fresh stitches where needed, and administered a broad-spectrum antibiotic injection while you slept. I certainly hope you're not allergic to penicillin."

"Not that I know of." She raised the hospital bed to a more comfortable position. "What about my friends? The two who were seriously injured?"

"Both are in surgery as we speak, but I believe they'll both make full recoveries given time." His reassurance was exactly what she needed to hear.

"Can I get you something to drink? Some juice perhaps?" the nurse asked, heading toward the door.

"Juice sounds wonderful. I can't remember the last time I had anything to drink."

The doctor's demeanor changed subtly as soon as the nurse left the room, his smile fading into something harder and more calculating. "You should have let things progress naturally up there, Miss Callahan. These hunting games have been a tradition in these mountains for two generations. You've disrupted something much bigger than you understand."

Before she could process the implications of his words, he pulled a syringe from his coat pocket. "I'm afraid the stress of recent events has critically affected your heart function. This injection will help stabilize your condition."

The realization hit her like a lightning bolt—he was going to kill her by lethal injection, finishing what Darryl and his men had started. But she still had some fight left in her, and she'd be damned if she'd die in a hospital bed after surviving everything else.

As he brought the needle closer to her IV port, she gripped his wrist with both hands and yanked her other arm free of the IV line, ripping the tape and causing fresh bleeding. In one fluid motion born of desperation and muscle memory from combat training, she wrapped the IV tubing around his neck and pulled him down on top of her.

He fought back viciously, his superior weight and leverage rolling them both off the narrow hospital bed and onto the cold linoleum floor. But Shea had the advantage of position and motivation—she wrapped her legs around his waist from behind. She maintained her stranglehold on the tubing, pulling tighter and tighter until the corrupt doctor began gasping for breath.

"Help! Someone help me." she screamed at the top of her lungs, struggling to keep his back pressed against her while maintaining pressure on his windpipe.

A nurse and security guard burst through the door within seconds. "What in God's name is going on in here?" the nurse demanded, reaching instinctively for Shea's hands.

"No, don't touch me!" Shea gasped. "He tried to kill me with that syringe he dropped. Check it—test whatever's in it. He's part of this whole conspiracy."

She refused to release her grip until the security guard understood the situation and properly restrained the doctor with handcuffs.

"We'll let the authorities sort this mess out," the guard said grimly, dragging the cursing, struggling doctor from the room.

"Back to bed with you right now," the nurse ordered, frowning at Shea's bleeding hand. "You've really done a number on that IV site."

"I needed the tubing as a weapon." Shea climbed back onto the hospital bed and drained the entire cup of juice in one long drink. "I don't need the IV replaced."

"Let me at least bandage that hand properly." The nurse worked with efficient competence. "I've always suspected something was off about Doctor Cooper, but I never imagined anything like this. You're one incredibly tough woman, Miss Callahan."

"All I want to do right now is sleep for about three days straight."

The nurse chuckled sympathetically. "I'm sure I can get Doctor Cooper's replacement to prescribe something appropriate for rest. I'll fetch a doctor who's been with us for a very long time—someone we can absolutely trust."

"Thank you," Shea murmured, already feeling drowsiness overtaking her again.

When she finally woke, she found herself in a regular hospital room with afternoon sunlight streaming through the windows. Sheriff Westbrook sat in a comfortable chair beside her bed, reading a paperback novel.

"How long was I unconscious this time?" she asked, her voice much stronger than before.

"It's the afternoon of the day after you were brought in," he replied, closing his book and setting it aside. "The medical staff thought you'd get better rest in a private room away from all the emergency department chaos."

"Do you have guards posted outside my friends' rooms?"

"We certainly do. The others who weren't seriously

injured are safely settled in a hotel under protective custody." He sighed heavily. "Darryl Hodges and his entire hunting party are behind bars, along with that doctor who tried to finish you off. I'm truly sorry your introduction to Misty Hollow was so violently unfriendly."

"You had no idea this hunting ring existed?" Shea asked incredulously.

"None whatsoever, but we've discovered that these men aren't actually from Misty Hollow itself. Now that we're aware of the recent developments, we're conducting a thorough investigation into missing persons reports from all surrounding towns and counties. I believe you and your friends are the first potential victims from my jurisdiction." He paused. "Are you feeling up to answering some official questions?"

"Yes," she replied, though her stomach chose that moment to rumble loudly with hunger.

The sheriff chuckled. "Let me find you some real food first." He left the room and returned several minutes later with a covered tray. "I hope you can tolerate hospital cuisine. Today's menu features a soy burger, sweet potato fries, and lime Jello."

"Why is there always Jello in hospitals?" She took a tentative bite of the burger and immediately grimaced. "This is terrible."

"You'll be discharged later today, otherwise I'd have one of my deputies bring you a proper meal from town."

"What's the latest on Tessa and Rachel?"

"Both came through surgery beautifully and are recovering well, which frankly amazes me given what they endured."

"Me too." They'd definitely had divine intervention watching over them. "Go ahead and ask your questions."

"Why don't you start from the very beginning and walk me through everything."

She began with their first encounter with Darryl at the gas station and the seemingly innocent detail of wearing matching pink shirts that had made them such visible targets. Then she relived the entire horror of the past few days, recounting each attack, the improvised traps, and the terrible necessity of killing three men in self-defense. By the time she finished the account, her appetite had completely disappeared, and she pushed the remaining food aside.

"What did you discover when you arrested the men?" she asked.

"Not much more than what you've already told me, unfortunately. Hodges does legally own that cabin property, which complicates matters. I'd burn the place to the ground if I could, but as it stands, it will probably just fall into disrepair. Hodges himself will be locked away for a very long time." He removed her tray and set it outside the door, then returned to stand beside her bed.

"Take several more weeks before officially taking

over my office. I can certainly wait that long. You need time to regain your physical strength and process what you've been through. But I want you to know—you did an outstanding job up there, Sheriff."

"I don't feel like I did such a great job. I killed three human beings. I'm not sure I'll ever be able to come to terms with that."

"You shouldn't be able to come to terms with it easily. Taking another person's life should never become routine or comfortable." The shadow that passed over his weathered eyes suggested he had his own regrets and difficult memories.

She nodded, understanding the wisdom in his words. "I have one more question that's been bothering me. Why didn't anyone run against me for sheriff? Nobody in Misty Hollow even knows who I am."

"Because I specifically recommended you for the position. After thoroughly reviewing your career record and talking to your former colleagues, I was convinced you'd be absolutely perfect for this job."

"I'm not sure whether you blessed me or cursed me with that recommendation." She found herself leaning toward the latter interpretation.

His smile widened with genuine warmth. "After what you managed to get yourself and your friends through up there, I'm completely confident you can handle anything this job might throw your way." He extended his hand for a firm handshake. "Welcome to Misty Hollow, Sheriff Callahan."

Epilogue

A month later, Shea and her friends stood over Melanie's grave. Silent tears poured down Shea's face. Things could've been a whole lot worse, but Melanie would be missed.

The funeral had taken place a couple of weeks earlier, but Tessa and Rachel hadn't been recovered enough to attend. So, the group had joined that day to pay their respects. Friends since college, now missing one.

"I still can't believe she's gone," Emma said. "The whole thing is like a nightmare that I can't wake up from."

"If not for Shea, it might be more of us lying in a grave." Annie dabbed her eyes with a tissue.

"We all did our part." Shea couldn't have done it alone. "After time, our girls' weekend away will be nothing more than a horrific memory." She hoped. "I start my job on Monday." As acting sheriff, she should have plenty to keep her mind occupied.

"Finally." Rachel smiled. "Life goes on or so they say. None of ours will ever be the same, though."

"While I'll never forget what those men tried to do to me." Tessa dropped a carnation on the grave. "I'm hopeful counseling will help me."

"On a good note, Bill and I have decided to try and work things out," Becky said. "After hearing how he could've lost me, he saw how much he still cares."

"That's great news." Deborah hitched her chin. "Let's not be strangers, though, okay? Maybe our next get-together can be on a cruise ship. No more woods or cabins for me."

They all gave nervous laughs and agreed.

"I'm going back to the cabin one last time." Shea glanced at each of them. "Any of you that want to come are welcome."

They all shook their heads except for Becky. "I'll come. You'll need moral support to confront whatever demons you're wanting to face."

She should've known her best friend wouldn't let her go alone. "I'm glad to have you."

"I'll follow you up." Becky unclipped her car keys from her purse. "That way, I can start the drive home when we're finished."

An hour later, Shea stood in front of what was left of the cabin that had been their prison. The front door hung open. Bullet holes marred the outside walls. Shattered glass from the windows lay on the porch.

Squaring her shoulders, Shea stepped inside. A

stain marked the floor where Melanie had laid.

Shea stood still and listened. Birds sang and squirrels chattered. Some woodland animal scurried from under the cabinets.

Just a house. No longer a place of torture and fear. Probably never would be again. The evil that had hung over the building had gone.

Becky stepped beside her and linked her arm with Shea's. "I hope they find the missing people who had stayed here before us."

"Me, too."

"You okay?" She cut Shea a quick glance.

"Yes, I think I will be. It isn't these woods or this house that threatened us. It was Darryl and his men. They can't harm anyone anymore." Darryl and his men would serve life sentences with no chance of parole. If others were found, more time would be tacked on to their sentences. None of them would ever see the outside of prison again.

Shea turned and left the cabin, leaving behind the signs of their struggle to survive. "Let's move on. We've got lives to get back to you." Thankfully. Things could've turned out so differently.

Becky hugged her. "I love you. When you've got some time, come have supper with me and the family. I can't bear to let too much time go without seeing you. What we went through tightened our bond, don't you think?"

"Yes." Although she wasn't sure about the others.

Some of them might not want to be reminded of their time up here. "I promise to call you once I'm settled."

Without backward glances, the two marched to their vehicles and drove away.

The End

Read the first chapter of book two, *The Threat*.

Chapter One

Shea Callahan lifted the small box of personal items and carried them onto the porch of the small ranch house she'd recently purchased. A note tacked to her front door stopped her in her tracks.

Squelching the urge to read it, she pulled it free and dropped it into her box. Already running late with new deputies to meet since all the prior ones had left with the retirement of the former sheriff, she wanted to be at the office bright and early. Whatever someone needed so urgently as to leave a note could wait a few more minutes. "Come, Heidi." Her German shepherd bounded after her.

She climbed into the driver's seat of the Ford pickup she'd traded for her sedan and backed from the dirt drive to start her new life as the sheriff of Misty Hollow. It wouldn't be easy. She'd already heard rumblings in town about whether or not a woman could handle the job despite her taking down a ring of evil men a few months ago and helping bring the mayor down for his crimes a few weeks ago.

"Welcome, Sheriff." Doris Belwright, the station's receptionist greeted her. "The new hires will be here by nine as you requested. Except for Deputy Sheriff Trevor Broderick who covered for us during the night. He's in the bullpen."

"Thank you." Shea passed through the bullpen. The desks were empty. She set the box of her things on her desk and surveyed the small space.

"Coffee?"

She whipped around, reaching for the gun on her hip.

A handsome man with hair the color of dark chocolate and eyes like the Arkansas summer sun held a mug toward her. "Welcome, Sheriff." He smiled, revealing dimples in both cheeks. His gaze dropped to her hip. "Don't shoot me. I give up."

"Sorry." She took the cup and set it on her desk before thrusting her hand toward him. "Sheriff Callahan."

"Trevor Broderick." He gave her hand a firm shake. "I didn't know if you took cream or not."

"Black is fine." Her gaze flicked to the box on her desk.

"Well then, I'll let you get settled in." He gave a nod and backed from her office.

Shea placed the mail on the desk in a pile to one side to go through after the morning meeting. She placed a photo of Heidi on the cover of her desk, her favorite coffee mug, and a pencil holder in the shape of a sheriff's badge that her best friend, Becky, had given her. That was it. All the personal effects of her office.

She plopped down in the leather chair behind the battered wooden desk. "This is where we'll spend a lot of our time, girl."

With a soft woof, Heidi moved from under her desk and jumped onto one of the two chairs across from Shea reserved for visitors. She'd have to get the dog a bed for the office.

By the time she'd checked emails, replied to the ones she could, and organized the work she'd dole out at the meeting, nine a.m. arrived. She motioned for Heidi to stay, then headed for the conference room. Thanks to a tour from the former sheriff, Westbrook, she knew where everything was.

"Good morning." Shea took up position at the front of the room and eyed the five men staring at her. "I've already met Deputy Broderick. I'm Sheriff Callahan. Please introduce yourselves." Since she'd gone through their files, she already knew their descriptions, ages, and their backgrounds, but having them tell her their names might break the ice before she gave them their orders.

"William Butler. Folks call me Bill," a man in his fifties said. Richard Bombeck was in his early forties. Lance Billings and Mark Cutter were both in their thirties.

"Thank you. I've posted the schedule for everyone in the break room. We'll all take our turn at manning the office during night hours." She hoped her smile hid her nervousness. "We've a slow morning as far as complaints go. I've got Cutter and Butler on tonight's shift, so the two others are free until then. Is everyone okay with three nights on and four days?"

Heads nodded devoid of smiles.

Her own smile faded under their stern expressions. It would take a while for her to earn their trust. "I want open communication between us, Deputies. If you feel uncomfortable for any reason, I want you to come to me. If you have a gut feeling about one of the cases assigned to you, I want to know. We're all partners here."

Her gaze landed on Broderick, the only friendly face looking at her. As deputy sheriff, he was one rung under her, hired by the former sheriff. Hopefully, she could trust him to have her back. "Any questions?"

"Yeah." Butler crossed his arms. "You ready for this job after what happened up on the mountain?"

She frowned. "What do you mean?"

He shrugged. "Takes a lot out of a person being hunted and killing men in hand-to-hand combat."

Out of a woman, he meant. "I wouldn't be here if I couldn't handle the job."

"She proved herself capable when she helped Westbrook bring down the former mayor." Broderick shot her a look, then locked gazes with Butler.

~

"Hold up, Bill." Trevor stopped the man before he left the building.

"Yeah?" He glanced back.

"You got problems with a woman sheriff?" Might as well get straight to the point.

"What makes you think I do?"

"Your attitude in the meeting."

"Dude." He smacked gum. "I'd have reservations about anyone new. She might be one tough cookie, but she's never been a sheriff before."

"The town voted her in on Westbrook's word. That's good enough for me." Trevor crossed his arms. "It should be good enough for you."

"I didn't know Westbrook either." Bill shoved open the door and marched from the building.

Trevor glanced at Doris. "This kind of behavior normal around here?"

"No, but the previous deputies all knew the man they worked for. Everyone here is new now except for me." She reached for the ringing phone. Before Trevor could return to his desk, she stopped him. "Accident on 105. You want it?"

"Sure." He stopped at the sheriff's office. "I'm heading to an accident. Want to join me? Let the folks around here see a bit more of you?"

She nodded. "Come, Heidi."

The dog he hadn't noticed earlier jumped from a chair and padded after her. "She friendly?"

"Unless I order otherwise."

"Guess I'll be on my best behavior then." He grinned. "I'll drive."

From her stony expression, he guessed she

preferred to drive, but she didn't argue with him. She opened the back door to the squad car and let her dog in, before climbing into the front passenger seat.

They made the drive in silence. The accident wasn't what Trevor had expected. Instead of two automobiles, a tractor and a hay bailer awaited them. Two men in denim coveralls stood toe-to-toe arguing and waving their arms.

Callahan's widened eyes seemed to flick from blue to green as she surveyed the situation.

"Didn't expect this." She shoved open her door and marched toward the two men, Trevor on her heels. "Gentlemen."

They turned as one. "Frank here ran right out of that field in front of me. Everyone but a fool knows I can't stop this tractor on a dime!" His hands curled into fists. "He punctured one of my tires."

"You were going too fast, Oscar. You should've seen me coming across that field."

Seemed to Trevor they both should've seen each other, since the sides of the road had nothing but freshly plowed fields.

Callahan circled the scene, her shrewd gaze taking it all in before she stopped next to the hay baler. "Can you back this up?"

"Yes, ma'am, but Oscar should have to be the one to move."

"Sir, the tractor is sitting on three tires. Until the flat one is repaired or we can tow it, the tractor isn't going anywhere. Deputy Broderick, will you direct traffic around this mess?"

"Yes, Sheriff." He took up position on the other side of the road and motioned cars through. A line of rubberneckers formed with every driver wanting to see what the commotion was about.

An hour later, the hay baler had returned to the field and the tractor was towed. Sheriff Callahan told the men to take up who was responsible with a judge since there were no witnesses, but both were at fault in her opinion. She'd handed them both tickets and returned to the squad car.

"You handled that well." Trevor grinned as he slid into the car.

"You didn't think I would?" She arched a brow, her eyes flashing.

"Didn't say that." Wow, she had a chip on her shoulder. He turned the car around and headed toward town. "I thought you were fair under the circumstances. I'd have handled it the same."

"Glad I have your approval." She leaned forward, peering out the window. "Stop the car."

He pulled over to the side. The sheriff slid down a ditch and returned with a calico kitten cradled against her chest.

"Poor thing would have gotten run over." She glanced around. "Hope you don't mind a friend, Heidi." She held the kitten so the dog could sniff her. Heidi gave a soft woof then lay down on the backseat.

Callahan smiled. "The sheriff's department now has a mascot."

Grinning, Trevor shook his head. The new sheriff had a soft heart after all.

Back at the office, leaving the sheriff to get the kitten settled, he returned to his desk and pulled up every article he could find on what had happened with Sheriff Shea Callahan on the other side of Misty Mountain.

When he finished, he sat back in his chair. The beautiful raven-haired sheriff seemed as tough as nails except for the dog and kitten. The way she'd reached for her gun when he'd startled her with the coffee told him she might be suffering from PTSD. Who wouldn't after what she'd gone through?

The question was…would that hinder her ability to do her job?

Dear Reader,

I hope you've enjoyed meeting Shea Callahan, the new sheriff of Misty Hollow. She's one tough cookie and more than a match for any trouble she might encounter in her new job. I can't wait to see what her next adventure brings.

Cynthia

www.cynthiahickey.com

Cynthia Hickey is a multi-published and best-selling author of cozy mysteries and romantic suspense. She has taught writing at many conferences and small writing retreats. She and her husband run the publishing press, Winged Publications. They live in Arizona and Arkansas, becoming snowbirds with three dogs. They have ten grandchildren who keep them busy and tell everyone they know that "Nana is a writer."

Connect with me on FaceBook
Twitter
Sign up for my newsletter and receive a free short story

www.cynthiahickey.com

Follow me on Amazon
And Bookbub

Shop my bookstore on shopify. For better price and autographed books. You can also subscribe to Mysterious Delivery, a mystery and suspense monthly book subscription with a book and several surprise goodies to pamper the reader.

Enjoy other books by Cynthia Hickey

Cowboys of Misty Hollow
Cowboy Jeopardy
Cowboy Peril
Cowboy Hazard

Cowgirl Blaze
Cowboy Uncertainty
Cowboy Christmas Crisis

Misty Hollow
Secrets of Misty Hollow
Deceptive Peace
Calm Surface
Lightning Never Strikes Twice
Lethal Inheritance
Bitter Isolation
Say I Don't
Christmas Stalker
Bridge to Safety
When Night Falls
A Place to Hide
Mountain Refuge

Stay in Misty Hollow for a while. Get the entire series here!

The Seven Deadly Sins series
Deadly Pride
Deadly Covet
Deadly Lust
Deadly Glutton
Deadly Envy
Deadly Sloth
Deadly Anger

The Tail Waggin' Mysteries
Cat-Eyed Witness

The Dog Who Found a Body
Troublesome Twosome
Four-Legged Suspect
Unwanted Christmas Guest
Wedding Day Cat Burglar

Brothers Steele
Sharp as Steele
Carved in Steele
Forged in Steele
Brothers Steele (All three in one)

The Brothers of Copper Pass
Wyatt's Warrant
Dirk's Defense
Stetson's Secret
Houston's Hope
Dallas's Dare
Seth's Sacrifice
Malcolm's Misunderstanding
The Brothers of Copper Pass Boxed Set

Time Travel
The Portal

Tiny House Mysteries
No Small Caper
Caper Goes Missing
Caper Finds a Clue
Caper's Dark Adventure
A Strange Game for Caper

Caper Steals Christmas
Caper Finds a Treasure
Tiny House Mysteries boxed set

Wife for Hire – Private Investigators
Saving Sarah
Lesson for Lacey
Mission for Meghan
Long Way for Lainie
Aimed at Amy
Wife for Hire (all five in one)

A Hollywood Murder
Killer Pose, book 1
Killer Snapshot, book 2
Shoot to Kill, book 3
Kodak Kill Shot, book 4
To Snap a Killer
Hollywood Murder Mysteries

Shady Acres Mysteries
Beware the Orchids, book 1
Path to Nowhere
Poison Foliage
Poinsettia Madness
Deadly Greenhouse Gases
Vine Entrapment
Shady Acres Boxed Set

CLEAN BUT GRITTY Romantic Suspense

Highland Springs

Murder Live
Say Bye to Mommy
To Breathe Again
Highland Springs Murders (all 3 in one)

Colors of Evil Series

Shades of Crimson
Coral Shadows

The Pretty Must Die Series

Ripped in Red, book 1
Pierced in Pink, book 2
Wounded in White, book 3
Worthy, The Complete Story

Lisa Paxton Mystery Series

Eenie Meenie Miny Mo
Jack Be Nimble
Hickory Dickory Dock
Boxed Set

Hearts of Courage
A Heart of Valor
The Game
Suspicious Minds
After the Storm
Local Betrayal
Hearts of Courage Boxed Set

Overcoming Evil series
Mistaken Assassin
Captured Innocence
Mountain of Fear
Exposure at Sea
A Secret to Die for
Collision Course
Romantic Suspense of 5 books in 1

INSPIRATIONAL

Nosy Neighbor Series
Anything For A Mystery, Book 1
A Killer Plot, Book 2
Skin Care Can Be Murder, Book 3
Death By Baking, Book 4
Jogging Is Bad For Your Health, Book 5
Poison Bubbles, Book 6
A Good Party Can Kill You, Book 7
Nosy Neighbor collection

Christmas with Stormi Nelson

The Summer Meadows Series
Fudge-Laced Felonies, Book 1
Candy-Coated Secrets, Book 2
Chocolate-Covered Crime, Book 3
Maui Macadamia Madness, Book 4
All four novels in one collection

The River Valley Mystery Series
Deadly Neighbors, Book 1
Advance Notice, Book 2
The Librarian's Last Chapter, Book 3
All three novels in one collection

Historical cozy
Hazel's Quest

Historical Romances
Runaway Sue
Taming the Sheriff
Sweet Apple Blossom
A Doctor's Agreement
A Lady Maid's Honor
A Touch of Sugar
Love Over Par
Heart of the Emerald
A Sketch of Gold
Her Lonely Heart

Finding Love the Harvey Girl Way
Cooking With Love
Guiding With Love
Serving With Love
Warring With Love
All 4 in 1

Finding Love in Disaster

The Rancher's Dilemma
The Teacher's Rescue
The Soldier's Redemption

Woman of courage Series

A Love For Delicious
Ruth's Redemption
Charity's Gold Rush
Mountain Redemption
They Call Her Mrs. Sheriff
Woman of Courage series

Short Story Westerns
Flowers of the Desert

Contemporary

Romance in Paradise
Maui Magic
Sunset Kisses
Deep Sea Love
3 in 1

Finding a Way Home
Service of Love
Hillbilly Cinderella
Unraveling Love
I'd Rather Kiss My Horse

Christmas
Dear Jillian

Romancing the Fabulous Cooper Brothers
Handcarved Christmas
The Payback Bride
Curtain Calls and Christmas Wishes
Christmas Gold
A Christmas Stamp
Snowflake Kisses
Merry's Secret Santa
A Christmas Deception

The Red Hat's Club (Contemporary novellas)

Finally
Suddenly
Surprisingly
The Red Hat's Club 3 – in 1

Short Story

One Hour (A short story thriller)
Whisper Sweet Nothings (a Valentine short romance)

211